Ponzi:

The Prince of Pi Alley

Ponzi: The Prince of Pi Alley
by M.R. Paxson

Copyright © 2015

Photo Credits: According to U.S. law, copyrights for most photos from prior to 1923 have expired and thus are in the public domain. We gratefully acknowledge and thank these sources: The Boston Globe, The Boston Post, Keystone View Co., Wikipedia, Harriet Ewing, Old-Picture.com and The Boston Public Library. In some instances, there is fair use of copyrighted material. We are always happy to make corrections, updates or include missing sources or information, and remove images inadvertently used where a registered copyright has been renewed.
You may contact us at books@relentlesslycreative.com

ISBN- 978-1-942790-01-3
Author's Website: http://monicarixpaxson.com

Published by Relentlessly Creative Books
Publisher's Website: http://relentlesslycreativebooks.com/
773-831-4944

Ponzi:

The Prince of Pi Alley

A Novel About
The Scam of the Century

by

M.R. Paxson

Dedicated with Love
to My Sisters

Amelia

&

Diana

Table of Contents

Foreword 1

Leaving Italy 3

Prohibition 7

A Lucky Day... 15

Something New 25

An Unlucky Day.. 29

Endings 33

Young Ponzi 39

Beginnings 47

Tricky Business... 53

Moving Along.. 61

A Window of Opportunity... 67

Ladies Rule 75

Care for a Cigar? 85

A Busy Day.. 91

Raising Cane.. 99

Money Back Guaranteed 103

Surprise! 111

More Surprises.. 115

Big Business 121

How Rude.. 125

The American Way...129

Taking the Plunge 133

Returns...139

The Big Night 149

Party Night 157

Opportunists 163

Bad Press...169

Good Press...173

Pi Alley Circus 181

Blow by Blow 189

Feeling the Heat...195

The Fix..201

Breakdown 209

Back Pedaling 215

Poor Rose...221

Just Borrowing...225

Special Edition 233

PostScript 239

About the Author..241

About Relentlessly Creative Books 242

Foreword

What follows is a work of fiction based on the historical events and people surrounding Charles Ponzi in Boston during 1918-19. While many of the events depicted here really happened, and many of the people really existed, this is a fanciful retelling designed to offer the story as a fictionalized historical novel, and not as a journalistically accurate history. Some characters are entirely fictional and others are composites of several real people.

It is with love, regard, compassion and a sense of humor that these characters are brought to life here once again. And although a great deal of historical research went into its creation, and some of the words are actually those that Charles Ponzi spoke as recorded in news accounts of the day and other public documents.

The photographs are intended to be evocative rather than literal, except for those noted that are actually a part of the historic account. Most of the photos were taken in the 1918-1920 timeframe and most are from the Boston area.

This was an era of great change and epic historic events, including the end of Great War, the flu epidemic that took even more lives than the war did, and the beginning of Prohibition.

The lives of women were beginning to change as reflected in the shift in fashion from the idealized Gibson Girls of the late 1800s to the bobbed hair and shorter dresses of the roaring 1920s. Perhaps this photo of writer Lois Long in her office at the *New Yorker* illustrates the "generation gap" best.

Writer Lois Long

Chapter 1

Leaving Italy

Early morning departures were not Carlo Pietro Giovanni Guglielmo Tebaldo Ponzi's style. The sad sky was still nearly lightless. No sun had yet appeared to burn off the early clouds of mist that roamed around the seaside docks like wandering ghosts and days without bright sunlight did not suit Carlo Ponzi.

Ponzi had been a University man who'd seldom arisen before noon, and although he was well acquainted with the dark, it was from the other side: the night. Ponzi and his friends had been far more interested in which cards their hand held or in scouting the young women who sat in the stage circle below their balcony seats at the opera, the better to evaluate their décolletage.

S.S. Vancouver

Chin up, young Ponzi marched ahead of a small party of escorts, most notably his bird-like mother, Imelda, and his portly, gray-haired uncle Louie. The prow of a large ocean-faring ship bearing the name S.S. Vancouver made an occasional appearance through the fog and mocking gulls skimmed through the air just overhead.

The tiny knot of people followed their leader, faces full of grim determination, to the ramps where passengers boarded and porters transferred luggage, checked tickets and directed the wealthy to the upper decks and the unfortunate downward to steerage.

As if on cue, Ponzi stopped and faced his mother as the ship's horn blasted to warn stragglers that it was time to board. Imelda's otherwise stern face was streaked in tears.

"Aw, Mamma, don't cry." Ponzi daubed his mother's tears with an impeccably white handkerchief he'd plucked from his breast pocket.

"You go so far away. I am an old woman. What if I die?" asked Imelda, sobbing on her son's shoulder and clutching him around his waist, certain that she'd never see her son again.

"Don't worry Mamma. I'm going to America. No one dies there," he reassured her. "I'll get rich and I'll send for you. I promise. You'll see. I promise."

"Can't you hurry it up?" murmured an officious voice from a short distance away.

Ship Boarding

Uncle Louie made his move. He opened his wallet, removed several bills and tucked them into Ponzi's breast pocket. "There's no need uncle..." Ponzi protested mildly.

"Take it," his uncle insisted. "Of course you'll need money in America."

Two police officers stepped to the forefront, each taking Ponzi by an arm.

"Go now," the obviously distressed uncle instructed. "Get on the boat and don't come back," he said as Ponzi's escorts shoved their prisoner toward a downward leaning ramp. "Don't ever come back."

Chapter 2

Prohibition

On a busy Boston commercial street, a taxi pulled up to the curb and Richard Grozier, a man in his thirties, stepped out, fumbled with the coins the driver handed him as change and shrugged on his jacket. His suit was disheveled, but the pocket watch he pulled from his vest to check the time gleamed and the gold chain was heavy beyond what was necessary to do the job.

Richard skirted around the cascade of stone stairs that climbed to the bronze doors that were the entry through the façade of The Boston Post. Instead he dove into the shadows of a side door that lead directly into the pressroom.

The presses themselves were behemoth monsters, clanging and hammering, digesting mammoth rolls of newsprint and pushing out great stacks of newspapers. Yet despite the clamor, this was friendly territory for Richard, the son of the owner and publisher, who'd practically grown up here.

As Richard ran down the central aisle, dodging carts loaded with the afternoon edition, the pressmen, wearing their four-cornered hats folded from yesterday's paper, greeted him with smiles, nods and thumbs up (since it was entirely too noisy to speak, at least not without shouting).

Newspaper Presses

Richard returned their greetings as best as he could as he juggled his briefcase, glasses and a handful of posies and dodged the many hazards on the pressroom floor.

At the other end of the pressroom gauntlet Richard opened a door emblazoned with gilded lettering stating "Copy Room" and after a near miss with a nearsighted copyboy coming the other way, he entered a room full of desks, cigar smoke and the clickity-clack of typewriters.

At the far end of the Copy Room, Henrietta, his father's longtime secretary was waving for him to hurry. The girls in the typing pool giggled as he rushed by trying to rescue his necktie that was threatening to trip him since it was just draped around his neck and one end was dangling to his knees.

"You've got to help me Henrietta. Really." Richard pleaded as he'd done so often before.

Henrietta tied his tie and straightened his collar with a motherly touch. "You're a bad boy Richard Grozier," she said as she took the handful of half-wilted posies Richard offered her.

"You're a peach," Richard replied giving the secretary a quick busk on the cheek. "Wish me luck."

Henrietta opened the door to the publisher's well-appointed office and Richard slipped in and took a seat in a chair against a wall, hoping that his tardiness would be overlooked.

The Boston Post publisher, Edwin A. Grozier, every inch the patriarch, was pacing the length of the office and muttering. "It's about time you sho.... Never mind. Your mother's expecting me."

"Yes father."

"I don't know what she finds so utterly fascinating about Cape Cod. Damn place is full of seagulls. You ever notice those beady yellow eyes seagulls have?"

"Yes father."

"Evil birds, I say, seagulls."

"Yes father."

"Which reminds me: What possessed me to agree to this?"

"I don't know father."

"If a story breaks, promise you'll send for me. Have Henrietta send a telegraph if you need to, but send for me."

"Yes father."

"Just because news is slow during the summer doesn't mean we lower our standards. Am I clear?"

"Yes sir."

"This is probably a huge mistake."

"Yes father," Richard agreed.

"God willing then, I'll see you at the end of August."

Father & Son

"Goodbye father. Have a safe trip. Best to mother."

Edwin Grozier, still muttering, left the office at last, but not without a final backward glance at his son and the shake of his head in disbelief.

Richard remained silently seated, glancing nervously from right to left, fully expecting that his father might have a change of heart about leaving Richard as the head of his empire for a few weeks and return.

Henrietta entered smiling and whispered conspiratorially, "The coast is clear." Richard broke into a grin.

"Henrietta, if you were to take a two-hour lunch today, I wouldn't even notice." Henrietta was all charmed smiles and gave a little wave as she turned to leave to take advantage of this rare opportunity.

"Oh, just one more thing," remembered Richard, causing the secretary to pause in her tracks. "Please send in Mr. Dunn on the way out."

Richard took a seat in the big leather chair behind his father's desk, leaned back and put his feet on the desk. "This is going to be amazing," he thought as he considered what he'd do next now that he was the publisher, at least for the moment.

A tap on the door announced his arrival. Edward Dunn, The Boston Post's City Editor, was a man in his late twenties and Richard's friend.

"Enter and meet your new publisher," ordered Richard, barely suppressing his glee.

"He did it?" asked Edward doubtfully as he flopped into a chair in front of the desk. "Joseph and Mary, he really left you in charge?"

"Yes, he did. Have a cigar." Richard ordered as he opened a humidor. They each took a stinky black plug and sniffed the unlit stogies as if it were glasses of fine wine. Richard struck a match, lit Edward's then his own cigar, inhaled and choked violently.

"Good lord, these things are dreadful."

"Life's like that," Edward pontificated wisely. "Things are never as good as you hoped they'd be... So what's next? "

Richard began to pace in a manner uncannily like his father's. "Edward, my man," he cleared his throat and his voice deepened. "I think there's an important story we've neglected to cover."

"There is?" asked Edward, smiling. "And that would be?"

"It's a dark and terrible time," Richard continued.

"It is?" asked Edward.

"Oh yes. It really is." Richard paused at the large window looking out over the city streets. "I could weep. Prohibition starts in just a few days. It's the beginning of the end."

"Ah, the end of your favorite pastime."

"True enough," Richard responded. "But isn't just me. Just imagine. No one will be able to enjoy a well-deserved beer at the end of a hard day's work."

"Yes, the pathos, the angst, the vain glory — a sad, sad story." Edward was feeling the pain now too.

"Precisely. It's an impending tragedy and we have a professional duty to describe how a perfectly lovely way of life is coming to an end."

"Duty calls, responded Edward, not entirely sure where this was going. "Should I get my notebook? Take some notes?"

"I think not," advised his new boss. "This requires undercover research. Meet the natives on their own terms. Yes, feet-on-the-ground is better for this kind of thing you know. Let's scram."

"Yes, let us," agreed Edward, and they prepared to follow the call of the wet and the wild onto the soon-to-be-dry streets of Boston.

Chapter 3

A Lucky Day

Things were abuzz in the Gnecco's kitchen. The family had gathered, as they often did, around the big circular table covered with a flowered oilcloth and a church-bazaar collection of wine glasses and cutlery. When dusk had fallen, candles were lit before the electric lights would be turned on. The scented candles added to the intoxicating mix of aromas in the steamy kitchen: oregano and rose water, garlic and the geraniums that sat on the windowsills.

Papa Gnecco turned the corkscrew to open a bottle of red wine with hands not quite as steady as they had been in his prime. But after sniffing the cork and pouring and savoring a taste, he pronounced the wine good and the crowd cheered as if their favorite team had just won a goal. Glasses were offered forth for filling and the food began to move from the stove to the already groaning table.

Rose Ponzi, a shy brunette with dark eyes, was two years younger than her more confident sister, Anna. Rose and her perennially worried mother, Mama Gnecco, served while Anna and her husband passed their dimpled baby back and forth. Papa's brother, Uncle John, scanned the sports pages in The Boston Globe, looking for his favorite team and grumbling when the scores were not to his liking. Rose, aglow with anticipation, jumped when the doorbell buzzed.

"It's Charles!" she announced as she scurried out of the room quickly followed by Mama Gnecco.

"What are they so excited about?" asked Anna of no one in particular. But everyone stopped talking and began to listen to the voices on the other side of the door.

"Good evening Mama. You look so beautiful," a man's voice effused. "Rose obviously got her loveliness from you. Look what I brought for you." Charles Ponzi knew how to please his mother-in-law.

"Oh Carlo! For me? Bellisima!" she exclaimed as the three entered the kitchen, Mama with an armload of daisies followed by Rose and Ponzi holding her hand. He doffed his straw hat, tucked it neatly under his arm and bowed.

Charles Ponzi

"Good evening ladies, gentlemen. And for my precious wife..." Charles Ponzi, now using the Americanized version of his name, produced a single red rose from behind his back.

"For you, my love, a perfect American Beauty rose. You're as lovely as you were the day I met you. I'm a lucky fool— but the luckiest day of my life was the day I met my Rose."

"I was holding an umbrella for a friend, an elderly woman of my acquaintance, while we waited for a streetcar in the rain. When it arrived, the car was quite full and a number of us were standing."

Ponzi's audience knew that a story had just begun and they settled in their seats to listen.

"At first, I just sensed her presence... like the angels were calling to me. Then I turned and, oh my, one glance at her — that picture of loveliness — her deep, dark, smiling eyes — and I was no longer able to remove my eyes from her."

Rose blushed, smiled and looked away.

Ponzi continued. "I have no idea how long I stood there looking at that girl. It was probably only a matter of seconds. It could have been hours and I wouldn't have known the difference. Time, space, the world and everything around me, except that girl, ceased to exist. Fortunately, my friend recognized her."

"Why it's Rose," she said. "She's one of my music students. I want you to meet her, Carlo."

"I told you. It was my lucky day," Ponzi assured his audience.

My friend was so kind as to introduce us. "Rose," she said, "it's so good to see you. Allow me to introduce my young friend, Mr. Ponzi."

"How perfect, I thought. Her name is Rose, and how like a rose she is."

"Carlo, this is Miss Gnecco," my friend continued.

"'How do you do?' Rose asked. 'She spoke to me!'" Ponzi's amazement at his good luck was still evident.

Rose Ponzi

"I'm doing much better now, thank you," I replied. "I made no effort to conceal how I felt. I didn't care who knew. In fact, I wanted the whole world to know that I had met the girl of my dreams. All the way to Somerville my eyes did not leave her for an instant."

When we got off the streetcar, my friend asked me, "So, what did you think of Rose?"

"I think she is wonderful." I told her. "I am going to marry her," I said.

My friend told me, "Why, Mr. Ponzi, you must be crazy!"

"I am," I told her. "I'm crazy about that girl."

"It was only eight months later when we actually were married, weren't we Rose?" Rose nodded and blushed.

"Whatever else may happen to me in the United States, Rose is the most precious gift America could have given me. Who could bear malice against a country that has been so generous as to place within my reach to pick, from a whole garden-full of beautiful flowers, such as American girls are, what has been for me the most exquisite of all blossoms. An American beauty — my Rose."

As Ponzi and his wife embraced, Papa lifted his glass. "To my Rosa and her lucky husband. Here's to your first year together as man and wife. Happy anniversary my children." Everyone lifted a glass of good cheer to the smiling Rose and Charles.

Soon after, a discussion began over coffee. "Can you believe it?" asked an incredulous Uncle John. "The landlord wanted twenty dollars more today. For this we went to war? To make the landlords rich?"

"We're crazy if we don't get rich too uncle. All it takes is one good idea. Just one. You want to make money? I can show you how, can't I Rose?" Ponzi smiled at Rose who nodded in agreement.

"Mama, Papa, everyone. We have some very good news to tell you," announced Ponzi. Everyone fell silent and looked expectantly. Rose reached for her husband's hand.

Mama Gnecco, unable to contain her excitement blurted out, "Oh Rosa. I told your Papa just today. You're gonna have a baby, right?"

Rose looked embarrassed and confused.

"Not yet Mama," explained Ponzi. "There's plenty of time for that. First, we've gotta get rich. In America anyone can get rich."

This notion was met with disbelief, for the hardworking Gneccos had expected to labor all of their lives just as their ancestors had done.

"Look Papa" Ponzi explained in a soft but excited voice. "I have a new business." Ponzi pulled a piece of stationery from his breast pocket and unfolded it showing that it bore a letterhead: The Trader's Guide, it said. "I got the idea," Ponzi continued, "when I discovered a journal that demands five-hundred dollars of advertisers for a single-page."

"That much? Unbelievable!" Uncle John was genuinely amazed.

"Of course, it won't be that much in my journal. Not at first anyway. We'll start by charging a good deal less. That's why advertisers will come flocking to me. Let me show you." Ponzi pulled a pen from his pocket and scribbled figures as he spoke.

"The other journal goes to ten thousand people, but I can easily double that..."

Rose could see that this conversation was not likely to end soon, but she had to intervene. "I'm sorry everyone. It's late. I have to get up early and the streetcar will stop running soon."

Boston Streetcar

Taking the cue, Ponzi arose and extended his hand to his father-in-law, then uncle. "Gentlemen, this business will have to wait for another day. I must escort my lovely lady home."

When they arrived home to their working-class neighborhood, the happy couple disembarked the streetcar beneath the light of a single street lamp and climbed the stairs. Ponzi unlocked the door and stepped into a darkened room and clicked the light switch. Nothing happened. He struck a match. Rose and Charles lit candles as they spoke.

"Didn't we pay the electric bill?" asked Rose? "I thought we paid."

"I'm sorry. I had to pay rent for the office," confessed Ponzi.

"I won't get paid 'til Friday," said Rose as she took a candle to the table where the bills were neatly stacked.

"If Uncle John invests in the business," said Ponzi. "Just a thousand dollars would be more than enough."

"Uncle John has his own problems," Rose responded, sounding protective of her uncle. "How will he make money at the restaurant when he has to close the bar?"

"All the more reason he should come in with me."

"We can't ask my family for money," Rose agonized.

"It's an investment," her husband replied.

"I can't pay everything!" And indeed Rose could not, for her modest salary would not stretch that far, and it had been months since her husband had generated anything but bills from his business venture. And so, she began to weep.

Ponzi embraced his wife and smiled. "Rose, Rose. My poor little pussycat. Don't worry. Everything will be okay. I promise." He wiped her tears with a handkerchief. "Come now. Give me a smile." Rose smiled.

Chapter 4

Something New

Richard and Edward walked down School Street toward Pi Alley and the entrance to The Bell in Hand. Richard was tipsy enough to play the tour guide convincingly. (They had been doing "research" now for several hours.)

"This way Mr. Dunn," said Richard, arm extended toward a storefront bar. "Here we have The Bell in Hand, another doomed watering hole."

"Oh my," replied Edward. "But I think we've done enough research for one night."

"Come on, come on. Just one more," Richard whined and pleaded. "We haven't spoken with any of the native women yet."

"Yes, but we've sampled plenty of native beer and I've got a morning deadline."

"Taxi!" Edward hailed a cab that had pulled into the alley to release Amy Newly, an attractive woman in her twenties. First Amy's shapely legs appeared, then her slim torso, and finally a friendly face framed by a head full of finger waves.

"Shhhh. Quiet. You'll frighten the natives," admonished Richard.

Amy giggled on her way into The Bell in Hand, turning her head back once to make certain she was still being noticed.

"Look, there goes one now. Let's follow her."

"Oh Joseph and Mary" Edward sighed. "You're impossible," and yet he followed Richard into The Bell in Hand.

Richard and Edward sat at the bar in the crowded Irish pub and it wasn't long before they learned that the woman they'd followed was a barmaid there when she arrived to serve them.

"And what will you two be havin'?" the smiling Amy asked with a slight Irish accent as she wiped down the bar with a rag.

Richard leaned toward Edward and in a loud stage whisper reminded him, "Didn't I tell you? The watering hole is the best place to meet the natives."

"Quick," said Edward, his plea directed to Amy, "let's put him out of my misery. A couple of drafts please, Miss...Miss...?"

"Newly," Amy replied. "Miss Newly."

Amy filled two mugs from the tap behind the bar as she continued the conversation with Edward.

Barmaid

"Newly?" asked Edward. "Newly what? Newly wed? Newly mown hay?"

"Amy," she replied. "Amy Newly," she smiled.

The drunken Richard wordlessly buried his head in his arms on the bar.

"My, you are bolloxed, aren't ya?" Amy giggled, moving Richard's beer mug safely away from his head.

"Just ignore him," suggested Edward. "I'll take him home." Edward stood and looked at Amy. "It was very nice to meet you Amy. I'm Edward Dunn and this is my boss. We're reporters researching a story for the Post on how Prohibition is going to change Boston."

"Oh, that reminds me." Amy scowled. "Soon I'll be "newly" unemployed." She placed a jar labeled "tips" on the bar.

"Would you care to contribute to my retirement fund?"

Chapter 5

An Unlucky Day

The grand proportions of the Hanover Bank were designed to impress even the wealthiest investors. But a run-of-the-mill riff raff like Mr. Charles Ponzi would almost never have entered the inner sanctums of this prestigious institution, especially the bank president's office.

Yet, there stood Ponzi at the receptionist's desk, neatly dressed in a fashionable suit and a freshly starched shirt with gold-colored cufflinks (if perhaps not real gold) having somehow entered this elevated place where he was breathing the same rare air as the bank president himself.

The receptionist hung up the phone and announced, "Mr. Chmielinski will see you now." She stood and gravely escorted Ponzi to the great bronze door that stood at the entrance of the president's office and opened it for visitor Ponzi and announced him.

Ponzi, hat in hand and chin in the air, extended his hand to Mr. Henry Chmielinski, a dignified man in his sixties who was seated upon a kind of throne behind a desk of epic proportions.

Banker's Office

"Good day Mr. Chmielinski," Ponzi offered.

"Do I know you...?" sniffed Chmielinski.

"I doubt it since my account here has never amounted to much," Ponzi confessed. "My name is Charles Ponzi."

Sensing that he was going to be the victim of an unreasonable request, Chmielinski got right to the point. "What may I do for you Mr. Ponzi?"

"I'm here to discuss the Hanover Bank making an investment in my publication, The Trader's Guide. I am prepared to offer an exceptional rate of return."

"Mr. Ponzi, are you asking for a loan?"

"It's more of an investment, actually, an extraordinary opportunity," Ponzi explained.

"How much do you require Mr. Ponzi?"

"I believe a thousand dollars should be sufficient," suggested Ponzi.

"And you have collateral I assume? Real estate or bonds, perhaps?"

"You'll have my good name plus a very good rate of course."

"I'm sorry Mr. Ponzi. We couldn't possibly make an unsecured loan."

Ponzi smiled with patient tolerance. "Your investment with me would be secure."

"We have our policies," followed by another presidential sniff.

"Is it your policy to pass up brilliant opportunities? Ponzi countered.

"It's probably happened before."

"It probably happens all the time," replied an increasingly less patient Ponzi. "Look, Mr. President. You act like you're the cock of the walk, but it's really clear to me: you're just a capon."

"Pardon?" Chmielinski was puzzled.

"A capon. A chicken without gonads. A roosta that usta." Knowing that he'd been refused, Ponzi saw no reason to hold back.

Chmielinski was insulted. "Good day Mr. Ponzi."

"Yes, it is a good day. But not nearly as good as the day will be when you regret your stupid decision."

Ponzi strode toward the door, stopped before making his exit, and made the sound of a chicken while swinging his rear side-to-side like a hen's tail as he walked out the door.

Chapter 6

Endings

The office of The Trader's Guide was on the second floor of the Niles Building, a non-descript six-story office edifice facing School Street near the corner of Pi Alley. Ponzi truly loved going to the office, climbing the white marble stairs, and seeing the words "The Trader's Guide" in gold lettering on a panel of frosted glass in the door at the entrance to the main office.

Ponzi stepped into the nearly empty office and hung his overcoat neatly on a wooden hanger and carefully placed the hanger back on the head of a nail in the wall near the door. Mrs. Crabtree, the only employee, sat at the only desk. Large plate-glass windows and a door partitioned off a private office at the front where on the other side were large windows overlooking School Street.

Secretary

"Good morning Mr. Ponzi," the pleasant middle-aged slip of a woman greeted her boss. "Here's your paper. And here's the mail." Mrs. Crabtree handed him a copy of the Boston Post and three envelopes.

Ponzi took the paper and mail without interest.

"There were two calls from Mr. Daniels this morning. He wants to know when..."

Ponzi cut her off. "I know what he wants Mrs. Crabtree."

"And the Five Cent Bank called about an over..."

"Spare me. Anything else?"

"No sir."

"Thank you Mrs. Crabtree."

"You're welcome sir."

"Mrs. Crabtree?"

"Yes?"

"Are you a poker player?" Ponzi asked.

Mrs. Crabtree started to laugh. "Me? Mr. Ponzi!"

"I'm not such a good one myself. In fact I lost everything I had playing poker on the ship over here. I never could figure out how that fellow took me, but I did learn a couple of things about poker."

"What was that Mr. Ponzi?"

"Three of a kind beats two pairs. And if you've got a losing hand, the best thing to do is fold."

"Mmm..." murmured Mrs. Crabtree.

"So, that's what I'm doing with The Trader's Guide."

"What do you mean Mr. Ponzi?"

"I'm folding. Tossing it in. Calling it quits."

"You mean you're quitting the business?" the woman asked.

"Yes. Due to circumstances beyond my control."

"Oh dear! I'm so sorry Mr. Ponzi. What should I do now? I suppose I should take my check and go?"

"Yes, you should go. But there won't be any check."

"But you owe me for two weeks!"

Ponzi reached into his pocket. "Here, take my carfare. You can't squeeze blood from a turnip Mrs. Crabtree."

"I never dreamed. How could you Mr. Ponzi?" Mrs. Crabtree burst into tears.

"Please, please, Mrs. Crabtree. I just can't stand another weeping woman today." Ponzi turned his back and walked into his private office.

Ponzi sat at his desk and tried to read the paper, but was distracted as he could see the now angry and distraught Mrs. Crabtree through the windows. She packed her meager belongings and slammed the door on the way out. She might have kicked the cat had there been one.

Ponzi stood and walked to the window and looked down on the street below. A group of well-dress men were standing on the steps of the Hanover Bank. They shook hands and lit cigars. That's where Ponzi wanted to be—a big shot, doing business and having plenty of money in his account at the big bank, smoking good cigars and mixing it up with the fat cats.

Businessmen on the Street

Mr. Ponzi wanted the American dream. He wanted it so badly he would do just about anything if only he could think what to do. But just when he felt that a worthwhile future might be within his grasp, it was, slipping through his fingers. Would he really have to settle for less and take a menial job like everyone else?

Chapter 7

Young Ponzi

Ponzi returned to his desk, opened the newspaper to the "help wanted" ads and drew his finger down the column: accountant, bookkeeper, cashier, dressmaker, hairdresser, janitor...

He could scarcely believe he was looking for a job yet again. Ponzi began to remember what it had been like when he first arrived in America. He remembered the crowded employment office filled with recent immigrants, like him, looking for work. There he was, literally just off the boat, standing at the front of a line of people after waiting for hours. Now was his moment, he thought. Now he would be given the job that would make him rich like all real Americans.

A tired and bored looking official on the other side of a counter called out, "Next." Ponzi stepped forward to the counter and placed his papers in the official's outreached hand. The official glanced at the papers and then looked up. "Have you ever washed dishes?" he asked.

"I attended the University of Rome for four years. I studied Latin and Greek. I speak several languages. I believe a clerical position or perhaps a librarian..."

But before he knew what had happened, our young Ponzi was in a restaurant kitchen up to his elbows in dishwater, still in white shirt and collar, but with the sleeves rolled up, and wearing a white apron. A busboy brought a pile of dirty dishes and unceremoniously dumped them atop an already huge pile on the counter next to the sink.

"Hurry up. More acomin'" the busboy warned him.

Despite the provocation, Ponzi smiled. "I told you. Stop rushing me. Now I'm going have to cut you out of my will. You can't say I didn't warn you."

"Big deal. You're not worth anything," replied the busboy.

"Not now, but I will be some day," asserted the young Ponzi.

But the mature Ponzi wasn't in much better shape and he could barely stand it. Here he was, a grown and married man living in a country where the streets were paved with gold... or at least life was good for those businessmen across the street, and what had he achieved? Nothing!

Ponzi left the help wanted ads and tried to think, tapping a pencil on the desk as he tried to do anything but remember his painful past. He turned the pages of his newspaper to the crossword puzzle and read aloud. "Twenty-one down. Five letters starting with "f" meaning 'better quality'."

Ponzi spells as he writes.

"F - I - N - E - R"

But as he filled in the little squares in his neat hand he remembered another job he'd had years before and how scary it had been climbing to the top of a rickety ladder thirty feet off the ground in front of a billboard reading "Salducci's Finer Foods" in giant letters. Young Ponzi's once impeccably white shirt was now covered in splattered paint.

As he inched from the left side of the billboard to the right on a narrow platform, using his lovely calligraphic handwriting to paint the finishing touches, another sign painter called him from the ground below.

"Hurry the hell up, will you? We're supposed to be at the crossroads by noon and you're making us late."

"Hold your horses. I'll be done in a minute," the young Ponzi yelled back.

"Aw, crap," muttered the sign painter. "Why do they always give me

41

the pain-in-the-ass eye-taliyons?"

Ponzi grabbed a paint bucket by the handle and stood at the top of the ladder peering downward. "What's a matter?" yelled the sign painter. "You ain't gonna faint again are you?" A stream of paint poured down onto his up-turned face.

"Thanks for asking, but I'm feeling just fine now," young Ponzi yelled down.

Sign Painter

Ponzi threw the newspaper in the trash with disgust. Now he had no one but himself to blame for his failure. What was wrong with him? Didn't he know anything that would help with this seemingly hopeless situation? Hadn't he learned anything?

Then he remembered something. He remembered another job he'd had as a young man.

Young Ponzi was now dressed in the dull greens of a janitor and he was leaning on his mop handle watching a man named Napoleon Hill speaking on stage from the wings. The speaker was a well-dressed, dignified, middle-aged gentleman standing at a podium.

Like a single dot of color in a world of black and gray, Hill was wearing a bright red carnation in his lapel and addressing an audience full of young men in caps and gowns. Ponzi realized that these were the new graduates at Harvard University where he worked.

Ponzi typically ignored the academic goings on around him at Harvard because he resented the fact that he felt he was better educated than the students were, yet he was treated like a second-class citizen by the teachers and students alike.

But for some reason, he felt a magnetic pull toward this man, this Napoleon Hill, and he listened as the speaker continued to hold his audience spellbound.

Author Napoleon Hill

"So, the secret to wealth and success in our great land is always the brainchild of an ordinary human. Whatever your mind can conceive and believe, it can achieve. Never underestimate the power of a simple original idea coupled with an effective strategy."

"Remember: this is America," Hill continued. "There was a time, not so long ago, when America itself was born from an idea: that mankind should be free to determine its own destiny. It is now incumbent on each and every one of you to put your precious education to work, not to toil endlessly at the labors of the past, but rather to generate the future through your own ideas. You must always remember, especially when things look dim: a single brilliant idea can change the world."

The audience broke into thunderous applause.

A news photographer's flash filled the theater. Ponzi himself tucked the mop handle under his arm and clapped enthusiastically. The curtain dropped. Napoleon Hill left the podium and stepped into the wings.

A young Edward Dunn, holding a notepad, pushed past Ponzi and approached Hill to shake his hand. "That was a great speech Mr. Hill. I've got to tell you, I'm a real fan of yours."

"Why thank you young man," responded Hill. "And you might be?"

"Sorry sir. My name is Edward Dunn, and I'm writing a story about you for my school paper."

"Aha! A budding journalist! Did you know that's how I started out? I was a reporter for a small town paper."

"I hope to be a real reporter someday—maybe even a famous reporter. Would you mind answering a few questions for my story?"

"I'd be happy to if you'll walk with me to my car."

Hill and Dunn walked away just as young Ponzi's boss appeared at Ponzi's side with a clipboard. "If you ask me, we could use a little less inspiration and a lot more perspiration. Okay swabbie, hit the deck."

Chapter 8

Beginnings

Ponzi felt a bit better, although nothing obvious had happened. He was still sitting at his desk, still puzzled about what to do next.

He opened one of the letters Mrs. Crabtree had given him. It was a collection letter. He tore it up. He opened the second letter, and tore that up as well. Finally he opened the last letter. The return address indicated it had come from France. He tore open the envelope and unfolded the letter. There was an International Reply Coupon pinned to the corner of the paper.

Dear Mr. Ponzi,
We have learned of your new journal, The Trader's Guide, and

would like to consider advertising in your publication. Please send us a sample copy.

Enclosed, please find an International Reply Coupon that can be redeemed at any post office for first-class postage.

Sincerely yours,

Yves Laurant

Laurant Et Fils, Exportateurs

Ponzi focused his attention on the International Reply Coupon. He unpinned it, held it up to the light, and stared at it.

International Reply Coupon

Ponzi then grabbed the newspaper out of the trash. He took a fresh piece of paper from the desk drawer and pinned the coupon to it.

On the paper he scribbled: Franc, Mark, Lire, Dollar.

Next, he pulled the newspaper from the trash where he'd deposited it earlier, and turned to the financial pages.

"Franc, franc, franc..." he chanted as he looked for the financial information about the French currency. Finding the current exchange rate, he turned from the newspaper, back to scribbling calculations on the paper.

Ponzi awoke early the following morning still at his desk. He raised his head from the desktop now covered with papers, notes and calculations. He smiled, rubbed his eyes and then literally ran out of the office and down the stairs.

Just outside the door to the office building a flower seller sat with buckets full of fresh flowers. Ponzi picked a red carnation, pinched off most of the long stem and tucked it into his lapel. Then he carefully selected the most perfect single pink rose and handed it to the seller.

"Good morning Mr. Ponzi," greeted the seller. "Looks like we're gonna have a fine day."

"It *is* a fine day," replied a beaming Ponzi. It's an extraordinary humdinger of a day. By the way, I'm going to need a fresh red carnation every morning."

"I'll make sure they're here for you," said the flower seller as he wrapped the pink rose.

"And pretty soon it will be roses by the dozen, too."

The flower seller looked surprised. "Glad to hear it Mr. Ponzi. Glad to hear it." The seller held out his hand for payment.

"Just put it on my account," said Ponzi as he turned to leave.

"But you don't have an account Mr. Ponzi."

"I do now," said Ponzi who walked away before an objection could be mounted.

Ponzi's next stop was the post office. He arrived early enough to avoid the crowds and was able to immediately step up to a postal clerk's window and hand the clerk the International Reply Coupon.

"What can you tell me about this?" asked Ponzi.

The clerk examined the coupon. "It's an International Reply Coupon."

"I know what it is. What can you tell me about it?" Ponzi asked again.

"You give it to me and I give you a five-cent stamp."

"But this coupon was purchased in France," Ponzi added.

"It doesn't matter where it came from. We see these things from countries all over the world."

Postal Clerk

"But the person who bought it in France paid less than half a cent for it and you're willing to trade it for a five-cent stamp?"

"Doesn't matter what they paid. You want your stamp?"

"What law allows you to do that?" asked Ponzi.

"I'm no authority sir, but I think it's some sort of postal regulation."

"Which regulation?" Ponzi pressed.

"Dunno. Let me see what I can find."

The clerk rummaged through a drawer, located a small booklet and thumbed through the pages.

"I think it's right in here. Yup, page thirty-seven." The clerk pushed the official-looking booklet through the bars of the grill that separated them to Ponzi. "Keep it. It's government printing," he offered.

Ponzi took the booklet and looked at the cover. "The United States Postal Guide," it read. "Thank you," Ponzi told the clerk. "Anyone who says postal employees are lazy and inefficient clearly never met you. My name is Charles Ponzi, and my business is the Securities Exchange Company. I'm looking for a good clerk. If you're ever seeking a new position, you can find me on the second floor of the Niles Building."

"Thank you Mr. Ponzi. I just may do that."

Chapter 9

Tricky Business

The next stop was Gnecco Brothers Fruits & Vegetables in nearby Haymarket Square. When Ponzi arrived on foot, Papa Gnecco was carefully arranging produce for display outside the shop.

"Good morning Papa. How are you today?" Ponzi asked.

"Carlo! Good to see you." He embraced his son-in-law. "She's in the office."

Ponzi stuck his head in the door of the office. "I'll bet you're wondering what happened to me last night."

"Suppose I am? Suppose I worried myself sick about you," a truly gray-faced Rose responded.

Italian Grocery

"I'm sorry Rose. I was up half the night thinking and I fell asleep at my desk. Please accept my apologies. It won't happen again."

Sensing that the worst was over, Ponzi stepped inside and handed his wife the rose. "I wish it were a bucket full."

"The electricity is still off," Rose reminded him, her face still clouded with anger.

"That isn't going to be a problem any longer. I have great news. We'll have plenty of money to pay all the bills. I finally figured it out. I know how we're going to get rich. It's going to really happen now. You can count on it. You won't have to work anymore and we just might have to buy that electric company."

"You found someone to invest in The Trader's Guide?" Rose asked.

"Not exactly, Rose. It's a new business. I've named it the Securities Exchange Company and it's going to be fabulous."

"What are you talking about? You aren't making sense anymore. I'm worried Charles. Papa and Mama are worried too."

"Trust me. Don't worry. It'll all work out."

The next stop in Ponzi's plan was to see the printer. When he opened the door a little bell rang and the printer looked up from the press. Ponzi removed a paper from his pocket, unfolded it and laid it on the counter. "I want certificates printed for my business on good quality paper. Here's what they should say."

Printer's Shop

The paper showed a layout of a certificate with blanks for the amount, date and signature and a receipt on the side that could be torn off.

"But the important thing," he continued, "is they must have a fancy border, like a stock certificate and each one must have a different number. Is this something you can do?"

"We can. How many you need?"

"How much for six hundred? Ponzi asked.

"That will be thirty dollars."

"Can you have them for me tomorrow?"

"No, but maybe the day after."

"Good, I'll be back to pick them up then."

"That will be half now and half when you pick them up," the printer explained matter-of-factly.

"I'm sorry. I forgot to bring my checkbook," said Ponzi, patting his empty breast pocket. "Can't I just pay when I pick them up?"

"I only take cash."

"Then I'm afraid I'll need to visit my bank."

"I'll be here."

"I'll be back." Ponzi walked out slamming the door.

Diane Newly, Amy's older, more glamorous sister met her sister on the steps of the Five Cent Bank. After embracing each other they walked arm-in-arm down the street chatting a mile a minute.

"So, these two gentlemen came into The Bell in Hand — reporters for the Boston Post," Amy told her sister. "They wanted to interview me about what I'll do when the bar closes down."

"What did you tell them?" asked Diane.

"I asked them if they needed an advice columnist. I've been dispensing free advice from behind the bar for two years and I'd like to start getting paid for it."

"Seriously, what are you going to do?"

"I don't know," said Amy, stopping in her tracks.

"At least you've been saving your pennies," Diane assured her.

"You know the blanket the bank gives you when your account gets to five-hundred dollars?" asked Amy.

"What about it?"

"At least I won't freeze to death," Amy giggled.

"You should come with me to Argentina. It's summer down there while everyone here is tramping round in the snow."

"You're going to Argentina? But you just got back from Paris!"

"Argentina is the birthplace of the tango... that... and Eduardo..."
Diane explained.

Women at a Sidewalk Cafe

"So, which is it? The tango or Eduardo?"

Diane ignored her. "I'm going as soon as I can afford a ticket."

"I swear you are gone in the head. You go to Paris to be a painter and come back a dancer."

"I adore it! The tango is the most heavenly thing there is to do on earth." Diane stopped and put her arms around her sister like a Tango partner and did a couple of steps. "If you tried you'd understand... That's it! You can teach the tango."

"I can't dance," Amy reminded her.

Latin Film Actor Gilbert Roland

Chapter 10

Moving Along

Ponzi, with a red carnation in his lapel, sat at his desk reading the International Postal Guide. Suddenly, two burly movers and their boss, Mr. Daniels, entered the main office. Ponzi leapt to his feet.

Daniels supervised as the movers picked up the desk previously used by Mrs. Crabtree. They held it in the air as Daniels and Ponzi spoke.

"Just what do you think you're doing?" Ponzi demanded.

"We're taking the furniture," Daniels answered plainly.

"Hold everything." Ponzi told him. "I need that furniture."

"Then you shoulda paid for it. It's been two months and I haven't gotten a bleeding nickel from you."

"I already paid you thirty dollars," claimed Ponzi.

"That was just a down payment. You said you'd pay me fifty more, five dollars a week. Here's the note what proves it." Daniels reached into his pocket.

"Don't bother. I know I owe you the money. Can't we talk about it? Have a seat."

Daniels glared at him.

"Go ahead. Sit down. There's no obligation. You still own the chair."

Daniels sat. "I've been calling you for days. You never wanted to talk to me then."

"Look, what if I just paid you?" asked Ponzi, getting right to the point.

"Okay, give me the money."

"I don't have it, but I think I know how we can get it."

"How's that?"

"It's simple really. I'll give you my note for two-hundred and fifty dollars and you give me a hundred and twenty-five dollars in cash and the old note."

"What? That's crazy. That doesn't do anything for me. I'd be out more to you to boot. Besides you never paid on the first note. Why would I trust you now?"

"This is a little different," Ponzi explained. "You'd get your money right away."

"How?"

"You have a bank account in good standing don't you?"

"Of course," replied Daniels.

Furniture Movers

"You'll take my note to your bank and they'll discount it by ten percent and give you the balance in cash. That would be two hundred and twenty-five dollars to you. So far you've only given me eighty dollars worth of furniture and a hundred and twenty-five dollars in cash. I already paid you thirty dollars for the furniture, which leaves fifty I owe. You'll have the fifty dollars for the furniture as cash in your hand and I'll have my hundred and twenty-five dollars. And, for your trouble there'll be an extra fifty dollars free and clear to put in your pocket. Not bad for few minutes work."

"How do I know you'll pay the note?" asked Daniels, unconvinced.

"I'll pay the note since I am determined to pay it," replied Ponzi. "But, it won't be your problem any more. The bank will have to collect from me. You'll already have your money. And I'll have the bank to answer to if I don't pay. You don't think I want that do you?"

"I suppose," he shrugged.

"Good, then it's settled."

The two movers put down the desk. "I'll just write up the note. You can give me a hundred and twenty-five dollars, and we'll be done with it."

A puzzled Daniels left the office with his crew. He looked back toward Ponzi's office in bewilderment.

"That fella sure can talk," he marveled. Then he patted the note in his pocket and smiled. "Let's break for lunch boys. I've gotta go to the bank."

Back in his office, Ponzi was smiling too as he counted the cash and before the end of the day certificates were rolling off the press.

Chapter 11

A Window of Opportunity

The sign on the frosted glass of the door entering the main office now read "Securities Exchange Company," and a crew of carpenters was noisily building a teller's cage.

Ponzi finished a telephone call on his new telephone, purchased on installments, while a window washer lowered himself into view in the street-side window. He hooked his safety lines to the sides of the window frame. Ponzi went to the window, and tapped on the glass.

"May I speak with you for a moment?" Ponzi asked the window washer through the glass.

"I can't hear you," the window washer yelled. "Open the window."

Ponzi raised the sash. "Good day sir. My name is Mr. Charles Ponzi and I represent the Securities Exchange Company." Ponzi extended his hand.

Window Washer

The window washer moved his squeegee to free his right hand and shook Ponzi's. "Jimmy DuPree here."

"Good day Mr. DuPree. I wonder if you might have a moment to help me. I need someone to listen to a bit of a proposition and tell me what you think. It will only take a moment and I'll be happy to share a good cigar with you for your trouble."

"You mean right here?"

"I thought you might be more comfortable if you came inside," suggested Ponzi.

The window washer climbed in and took a seat. Ponzi offered him a cigar and lit it.

"I want to impress you with the notion that I'm only asking you to listen Mr. DuPree. I figure you to be a hard-working man, and like those of us for whom the dollar is dear, I'll bet you're reasonably careful about how you spend."

"I am when I have a dollar." DuPree grinned.

"Perfect. Then I'm eager to hear what you think. To begin, if someone has been fortunate enough to collect a few dollars, the next challenge is to keep it safe, and if you are lucky, to watch it grow. Thousands of people do this every day by taking their hard-earned cash to the many banks that line our streets, like the Hanover Bank over there or the Five Cent Bank on the corner. You yourself may have an account of some sort."

"I hope to," DuPree acknowledged.

"That isn't important. What's important is that you understand the concept of earning interest." Ponzi lit his own cigar and leaned back in his chair.

"You mean the money they give you for using the cash you put in the bank?" asked DuPree.

"Precisely. Are you familiar with the rate of interest these banks pay their depositors?"

"I dunno. Three or four percent I'd guess."

"That's correct," confirmed Ponzi. "And it takes a full year to earn that much. However, what most people don't know is that these very same banks are robbing them! For example, did you know that the bankers themselves are using the depositor's money to earn rates far in excess of what they are paying out in interest? It isn't unusual for a banker to be earning fifty, one hundred, even two hundred percent — enriching themselves greatly in the process. I myself feel that this isn't fair. The little guys in this world should catch a break too, if you know what I mean."

DuPree thoughtfully nods in agreement.

"That is why the Securities Exchange Company is prepared to pay a great deal more to those depositors who hold our certificates," Ponzi continued. "In fact, we are paying a full fifty-percent interest in only ninety days."

DuPree leaned forward in his seat. "Gee, that's great, but how can you afford to do that?"

"It's simple really. We can afford to do that because of a little-known fact about this little piece of paper." Ponzi held up an International Reply Coupon.

"This is an International Reply Coupon. They can be purchased in postal offices throughout the world. They allow the buyer to prepay the postage for a reply to someone in another country. All they do is tuck it into the letter they are sending to the other person. The person who receives the coupon can exchange it for a first-class stamp in his or her own country."

"Makes sense, I guess, but how can you make money with that?" DuPree wondered.

"A very good question Mr. Dupree. Consider for a moment the difference in the cost of the coupon and the value of a first-class stamp. If someone were to buy a coupon in Italy, for example, they would pay 30 centesimo. While that may sound like a lot of money, it is in fact, according to today's newspaper, only worth one and a half cents. But that same coupon can be exchanged here in Boston at any post office for a five-cent stamp. That, sir is a two hundred and thirty-three percent return on investment. With a return like that is it any wonder we can afford to pay our investors fifty percent?"

"But what would I do with all of those stamps?"

"Not stamps, sir. Cash. The Securities Exchange Company not only has representatives who buy coupons for us in Europe, we are able to sell the stamps we receive. Although I'm not at liberty to name names, I will tell you, many top-notch organizations see the value of purchasing postage for a discount."

"Oh, I get it. Impressive. But is this legal?"

"Perfectly legal. It's all covered here in the United States Postal Guide." Ponzi tapped the official looking document on his desk.

"So what do you think Mr. DuPree? Does this sound like something you could invest in?"

"Well, sure. It sounds great. But I've gotta tell you straight out. I don't have any money to invest."

"One of the beauties of our certificates is that they are available in any denomination. We can give the same excellent rate of return on ten dollars or ten thousand."

"I'm sorry Mr. Ponzi. I'm flat broke."

"I understand. But if you had money, would you be interested?"

"Hell yes! I even think some of the guys down at the pool hall might want to know about this."

Pool Hall

"You know," Ponzi spoke slowly, as if this were just occurring to him, "I have an idea. Perhaps there's a way you can make some money to invest. Now that you understand, perhaps you'll be able to make some money by working for us on the side."

"Sure, I'd be interested."

"Good. After all, this is America."

Chapter 12

Ladies Rule

The sign in the window of the tiny dance studio proclaimed that "world famous" dancer Eduardo, direct from Argentina, was teaching tango. And indeed he was. First he bowed to Diane Newly, took her hand, led her to the center of the dance floor and the bandoneón player in the corner began the slow, heartbeat-paced surges of the tango.

While it was still morning and the sun's rays were slanting through the front window casting a silver rectangle on the wooden dance floor, Diane Newly was dressed in floating silk, and the dancers moved so erotically, the passion so genuine, that Amy, the only audience for this performance, put her hand to her brow, as if to shield her eyes from the bright light. But the truth was that it embarrassed her to watch the lovers in action.

When the dancers ended with a flourish, Amy, sitting on the sidelines in a dress that might have been more appropriate for a tea party, applauded politely.

Bandoneón

"See what I mean?" exclaimed an excited Diane. "Pretty fabulous huh? Okay. He's all yours." She let go of Eduardo's hand.

Eduardo turned and just stood there, viewing Amy from head to toe, eyes hooded, breathing visibly from the exertion of the previous dance. The look on Amy's face was one of pure terror. The music began again and Eduardo approached slowly, step by sensuous step, and offered Amy his hand. She took it timidly and stood.

"There's nothing to be frightened of," Eduardo assured Amy. "Just trust me... And if you don't trust me, just pretend you do." He placed his arms around her, but held her at a distance and the dance began.

"It starts slowly at first," Eduardo instructed. "You are in control, aloof, distant. Quick, quick, slow, quick, quick, slow. Then..."

Eduardo dipped Amy backwards, surprising her into surrender.

"Oh my god!"

Tango Dancers

It was early morning in the office of the Securities Exchange Company in the Niles Building as well. Sunlight streamed through the windows casting a halo of light around the pert 18-year-old in a suit with hat and gloves, sitting on the edge of her chair across the desk from Ponzi. The teller's cage is complete.

"That's right Mr. Ponzi. I just graduated from the Bennett School."

"And what are your plans Miss Melli?" Ponzi asked.

"You can call me Lucy. I'm looking for a challenging position where I can do all the things I learned in business classes."

"And what did they teach you in business classes?" The interview continued.

Lucy began to enumerate on her fingers. "How to type, take dictation, answer the phone, set up files, and compose letters. I also learned bookkeeping and how to prepare an invoice. And, I can fold a business letter exactly in thirds."

Ponzi is charmed. "But you don't have any experience," he said.

Lucy pulled items out of her purse as she spoke, laying them one-by-one carefully on Ponzi's desk.

"No, but I do have a very nice letter of recommendation from Sister Maria Angelica at the Sacred Heart Academy where I used to be head girl. I also got this rosary – blessed by the Holy Father himself – for perfect attendance and here's a fabulous picture of God they gave me for winning the spelling bee. I really think I'm qualified Mr. Ponzi."

Ponzi is sold. "When can you begin?"

"When would you like?"

Through the window of Ponzi's office the occupants saw Jimmy DuPree enter the main office.

Young Girl's First Communion

Ponzi stood. "Now. Please come with me," he asked Lucy. "I'd like you to meet one of our salesmen."

"Good day Mr. DuPree," Ponzi beamed as he shook the man's hand. "Meet Miss Melli, our office manager."

"How do you do?" Lucy asked politely.

"Well, I have a little problem." DuPree emptied a wad of cash from his pocket onto the nearby desktop along with a pile of certificate receipts.

"This doesn't look like a problem to me," said Ponzi.

"I've run out of certificates," said the former window washer.

"Miss Melli, please put the cash in the drawer at our teller's window and record the receipts in the ledger you'll find there. Then, you'll need to get more certificates for Mr. DuPree."

Lucy neatened the piles and then stepped away with the cash and receipts.

"By the way," said Dupree, "if you still need help, I've got a couple of friends that want to be agents."

"Well, they're in luck. We're still expanding. I expect we'll be doing quite a bit of expanding."

It was also morning in the Publisher's office at The Boston Post where Richard stood in the middle of the room twirling a handsome black cane with a gold handle. Edward was perched on the edge of the desk nearby.

"What do we have for the lead story?" Richard asked.

"We've gotta go with the lover's triangle murder story again. Our readers love it and best of all, it's true – more or less," Edward replied.

"Yes, but we led with that story yesterday."

"We could go with "Houdini Escapes," but he always escapes," suggested Edward.

"Can't we dig up a really juicy scandal?" asked Richard, now tossing the cane from hand to hand.

"One of the pressmen just offered to give me a fifty-percent return on my investment in ninety days. That's pretty juicy," said Edward.

Richard looked at his watch.

"I don't have time to think about this. We'll go with the murder. I've got to give an award."

Richard tossed the cane and Edward caught it and examined it, feeling its inviting heft in his hand.

"Nice cane," he remarks.

"It is rather, isn't it? The gold knob is embossed with the name of The Boston Post. It's a little promotion father came up with: 'The Boston Post Cane.' We give one to the oldest living resident of each community in our region. It's good public relations – with a nice photo for the paper, of course."

Henrietta stuck her head in the door.

"The Abernathy's are here for the presentation Mr. Grozier."

"Good! Please send them in and fetch a photographer. Thank you Henrietta."

A group of relatives pushed their ancient grandmother into the room in a wheelchair closely followed by a photographer.

"Welcome to The Boston Post Mrs. Abernathy," Richard said bowing with formality. "The rest of you, please gather around your grandmother for the photographer."

The family members shuffled around. Richard cleared his throat.

"On behalf of all of us with The Boston Post, we are happy to respectfully award to you this beautiful token, honoring your extreme longevity: An official Boston Post Cane."

The Boston Post Cane

Richard, with solemn dignity, offered the cane to the grandmother.

The photographer yelled, "Smile"

The grandmother complained, "Idiot. What the hell do I need a cane for? Can't you see I'm stuck in this damn wheelchair?"

Edward, smiling, backed out the office door as the camera flashed.

Chapter 13

Care for a Cigar?

Ponzi was on the phone, but he could see through the windows that three customers were in line at the teller's window. The teller was the former postal clerk. Lucy sat at the desk where a sales agent counted a pile of cash onto the desktop.

"Rose," Ponzi spoke into the phone, "Put on your prettiest dress. Let's go to Uncle John's tonight to celebrate. Papa and Mama too."

Uncle John had purchased the restaurant where he'd worked as a cook when he first arrived in America. The owner had died and his wife was unable to manage both the restaurant and her twelve children. So Rose's uncle bought the place and soon was dishing out even more of the lasagna and manicotti he was known for.

As the Italian community grew and prospered, Uncle John added an adjacent standing bar for men only, as was the custom, although it was a family restaurant. But when the men departed for the hard stuff after dinner, the women gathered around the tables in the dining room for dessert wines and conversation. The bar was popular, but its days were numbered.

Ponzi, Rose, Mama and Papa Gnecco and the rest of the family were seated at a large round table in the crowded dining room. Ponzi stopped a passing waiter. The meal was over, but for one more thing.

"And a bottle of Sauterne with the dessert," Ponzi told the waiter and then turned to his father-in-law. "Papa, let's you and I go for a cigar while we wait." He stood and made a slight bow in the direction of Mama Gnecco. "Excuse us ladies."

Since the Italian immigrant community was tight knit, the bar was crowded with men who were well known to the Gnecco family.

Uncle John was behind the bar assisting the bartender.

Ponzi stopped to shake hands with one of the patrons. "Mr. Gonelli, nice to see you. Care for a cigar with us at the bar?"

Ponzi reached into his breast pocket and removed a cigar that he handed to Gonelli. Gonelli sniffed it, smiled and nodded.

"Havana?" he asked.

"My own special blend," Ponzi replied.

Ponzi turned to shake hands with Mr. Manzoni, who greeted him warmly. "Carlo. You're looking well!"

"I am well Mr. Manzoni."

"We haven't seen so much of you lately."

"You'll be interested to hear what I've been doing. Join us at the bar for a cigar?" Ponzi pulled a cigar from his pocket and offered it to Manzoni.

Gentlemen's Standing Bar

Uncle John carefully examined the cigar Ponzi handed him. "You still looking for investors for that... what's it called?" he asked.

All eyes were on Ponzi. The conversation around him subsided.

"My business is called The Securities Exchange Company. And no. We are not looking for investors, if you mean partners who invest for a stake in the business. We have all the funding we need. Of course, people who hold our certificates earn interest."

Charles Ponzi

Surprised and curious, Uncle John asked, "You paying interest? Better than the banks?"

"The banks can't compete with us," Ponzi smiled

"How much you pay if you don't mind," asked Manzoni.

"I don't mind, but I must warn you," Ponzi said, playing up the drama, "we only have a limited number of certificates available at this rate. We pay fifty-percent interest in ninety days on any amount, from ten dollars to ten thousand."

"Amazing," was Manzoni's stunned reaction.

"What? How can you do that?" asked the bewildered Uncle John.

"Simple Uncle. We make a great deal more than that... So much we can afford to reward our investors well. And it's all based on this."

The magician Ponzi pulled an International Reply Coupon from his sleeve.

Chapter 14

A Busy Day

On the way into the Niles Building, Ponzi took a red carnation, stuck it into his lapel and strode inside. As he was climbing the wide marble stairs, a line of people impeded his progress.

"What's going on here? Is there a problem?" Ponzi asked no one in particular.

The last man in line turned to him, "No problem," he said. "We're waiting to get into the office on the second floor."

"Why?" Ponzi asked.

"Some damn fool is practically giving money away,"

"Fifty-percent interest in ninety days," added a woman a bit further ahead. "Can you believe it?"

When Ponzi got to the entrance of the main office, he met Mr. Manzoni on the way out. There were lines of people at the teller's window.

"Let me shake your hand," said Mr. Manzoni, offering his. "This is quite an operation you've got."

"Yes, I'm a busy man," replied Ponzi, a bit surprised himself that his plan was working so well, so quickly.

"Well, I won't keep you. I've got my certificate. Thanks for telling me." Manzoni left a happy man.

When Ponzi stepped inside the main office, a smiling Lucy was standing there, waiting to hand him several messages. "We've been busy this morning," she advised him.

"How much money?" Ponzi asked.

"One-thousand and fifty-two dollars between eight and eleven," came her reply.

"You'll need to hire two more tellers. Maybe the postal clerk has friends. I'll call the carpenters."

"Will do Mr. Ponzi," she said crisply, obviously eager to fulfill the mission. "By the way, that top message is from someone who'd like to open a branch office."

Which reminds me Miss Melli, you'll need to set up a system for managing the branches — bookkeeping and so on. I'll take care of the foreign operations — buying the International Reply Coupons and selling stamps myself, but you are in charge of domestic operations."

"Sounds great Mr. Ponzi!"

"Come with me please. There's something I want to show you," instructed Ponzi as he led Lucy into his office. Ponzi removed a small stack of bankbooks and placed them on the desk.

"I've opened accounts at various banks. Here are the account books. At the end of each day you'll need to prepare the deposits. You can divide the money between the various banks by depositing into a different one each day. All except this one."

Ponzi held up the bankbook for the Hanover Bank. "Make a deposit into the Hanover Bank every day. Not too much – let's say just a thousand dollars for now. I want to build up the account, but not too fast."

Mr. Manzoni, fresh from his visit to the Securities Exchange Company, with a certificate in his pocket certain to earn far more interest than

he'd ever gotten before, sat down next to another patron at the stand
of a shoe shine boy in Haymarket Square.

Certificate Signed by Chas. Ponzi

"I gotta tell you," Manzoni confessed to the customer at his elbow. "I'm
feeling pretty good today. Just bought myself a certificate from the
Securities Exchange Company."

"So?" said the man, feeling a bit annoyed.

"They're payin' me fifty-percent interest in ninety days," explained
Manzoni. I don't know any bank that'll do that."

The man next to him was suddenly very interested. "Really?" he said.
"Do tell."

It was less than an hour later when the shoeshine customer Manzoni
had spoken to was sitting at the lunch counter in Woolworths waiting

for his tuna fish sandwich and flirting with the waitress in a heavily starched pink uniform like he did every day.

"Here's a tip for ya sweetie. How'd ya like to double your money in six months?"

"You're yanking my leg, right?" replied the waitress, accustomed to being teased.

Woolworth's Lunch Counter

"Nope. I'm dead serious. Check out the Securities Exchange Company in the Niles Building. They're paying fifty percent interest in ninety days."

On the way to the bus after work, the waitress, now out of her pink uniform, stopped to buy a paper like she did every day, but this day she was the one with news for the newspaper seller. "Believe it or not, you can get fifty percent interest in ninety days, on any amount you come up with," she told him.

Twenty minutes later, his regular customer, the one who played the ponies arrived at the newsstand and asked the seller, 'Ya got any tips on the ponies?'

"I got better," the news seller bragged. "How'd you like to double your money? Risk free."

Before long, the pony player had his bookie on the line. "Bernie, you're not gonna believe this.,. Fifty percent, no questions asked."

"Fifty percent?" responded Bernie. "Yeah? ...Whoa."

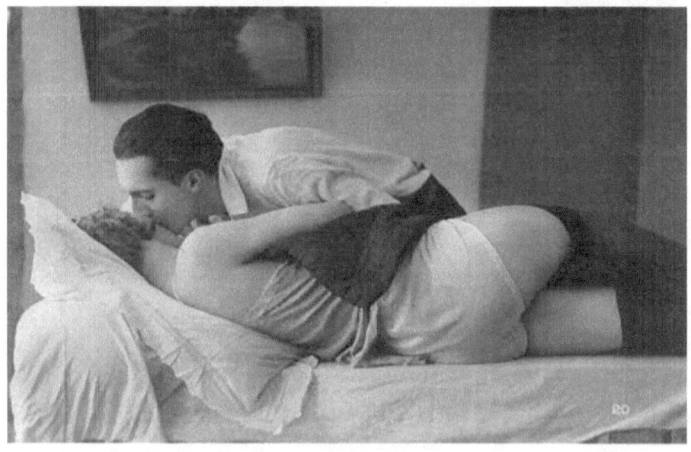

Pillow Talk

Bernie the Bookie took his girlfriend, to her favorite cheap hotel for a little pillow talk if you get the drift. They hadn't been in bed for five minutes before his girlfriend was yelling. "You gotta be kidding. Fifty percent? Bernie! You're a bookie! That could put you outta business!"

The bookie's girlfriend felt the need of a little touch up after her night of entertaining Bernie, but as she was sitting in the hairdresser's chair, she wanted to share a really big piece of gossip with the hairdresser like she usually did. But this time there was no one who got the cement boots or anything like that. She had something better! So she spilled the beans. "That's what Bernie told me," she said. "That guy Ponzi's paying fifty percent!"

The hairdresser was impressed. "Really? Amazing..."

When Diane Newly sat in the hairdresser's chair later that afternoon, she heard the latest gossip too. "So they're paying fifty percent in ninety days—I swear— right over in the Niles Building on School Street."

"Helloooooo Argentina!" Diane told the world when she realized that she'd have enough for a ticket in ninety days.

The printing press was running again, rolling off more fancy certificates for the Securities Exchange Company, but Ponzi was nowhere near. Miss Melli would be handling such trivial things from now on.

Lucy Melli

Ponzi was being fitted for his new suit of the finest fabric imported from Europe. The tailor marked the length of the legs, making certain that the cuffs fell just so over the tops of his shoes the way Mr. Ponzi liked them. Ponzi was standing in front of the mirrors, studying his image in all three reflections and lovingly fondling a fine black cane with a gold handle.

Chapter 15

Raising Cane

News may come and news may go, but the all-important promotion that was The Boston Cane was what concerned Richard Grozier at the moment. After all, it was rather nice having his picture in the paper with the title "Acting Publisher" in the caption. So he waited with anticipation, twirling the heavy stick like a baton until Henrietta announced, "They're here!"

"Send them in," Richard ordered.

A grey-haired man slowly ambled in with his even more elderly mother on his arm. Both the photographer and Edward Dunn, who waited on the sidelines for an opportunity to speak with Richard, followed them.

The mother looked around the office in bewilderment. "Is this the surprise you've been promising me?" she asked.

"Yes mother," replied the son. "Mr. Grozier is going to give you an award."

"Whatever for?" she asked suspiciously.

Richard took this as his cue. "On behalf of The Boston Post, I'd like to bestow upon you this beautiful Boston Post Cane to honor you as the oldest member of your community." There, he thought, things had gone well so far. "Now if you'll just smile for the photographer as I hand you the cane," he suggested.

"Give me that cane!" She grabbed the cane. "Are you out of your cotton-picking mind?" She lifted the cane and using both hands, attempted to bring a blow down on her poor son's head. "Do you think I want everyone to know old I am?"

Through quick action on Richard's part, the blow was diverted. (But the photograph that was to appear in the evening edition, relegated to page 18 rather than the traditional second page, was quite blurry.)

"Madame!" "This is an honor!" admonished Richard.

"If you print a word of this I'll knock your block off," she continued to yell, now threatening to hit Richard with the "honor."

Edward could barely contain his glee. "Maybe some other time..." he mumbled as he backed toward the exit. "I'm off to see a man named Ponzi. It sounds like a good story. See ya."

Edward escaped.

Chapter 16

Money Back Guaranteed

When Edward arrived at the Niles Building, the first thing that he noticed was that a policeman was posted at the entrance.

"If you're going to the Securities Exchange, please keep to the right." The officer was directing traffic.

Once inside he understood what the issue was, there was a line of people, all kinds of people, snaking up the stairs. There were businessmen in suits and straw hats and recent immigrants wrapped in the shawls that were so ubiquitous back in the old country, there were shop girls and paper boys, there was even a pretty young woman that reminded him of a taller version of Amy Newly without realizing that it was Amy's sister Diane.

When Edward, who had an appointment after all, decided to skirt the line, a young man in a uniform attempted to block him. "What's your hurry Mister?" he asked.

"Take your money to the end of the line like the rest of us," insisted a businessman with a monocle.

"That's right. We were here first," came a chorus of protests.

School Street

"I'm not here to invest. I'm just here for an interview. Please let me through," Edward explained.

"An interview? With Mr. Ponzi?" asked someone in the crowd. Edward nodded. "Big shot comin' through. Let the man get through."

In the main office, a line of customers stood at each of the three teller's windows and there was a new typist next to Lucy's desk.

Edward knew immediately that Lucy was the "go to" girl and approached her. I'm Edward Dunn with the Boston Post, here to see Mr. Ponzi. Lucy guided him into Ponzi's office.

Ponzi rose from his desk and extended his hand. "Welcome to our humble office Mr. Dunn. I see that you've already met Miss Melli. The girl is a gem. Runs the place I tell you."

"Oh Mr. Ponzi!" Lucy blushed.

"Please have a seat Mr. Dunn"

Ponzi, still standing, watched through the window into the main office where the lines of people waited. "Look at that Mr. Dunn. Lined up they are. I tell you, America is the greatest country in the world."

"I've had a number of people tell me about your business," Edward began, notes at hand.

"All good news I hope."

"They tell me you're paying a lot of interest."

Ponzi paced to the other side of the office and looked out the window looking down on the street. "See that bank on the corner? It's a very successful operation. The people who own stock in it have grown wealthy on depositor's funds, but what do they offer the person with a small account?"

Journalist

"They pay interest just like any other bank," replied Edward.

"Yes, the fewer pennies the better. Let me put it another way. Has a bank ever turned you down?"

"You mean for a loan?"

"Not a proud moment was it? Almost everyone in that office out there has suffered that indignity or worse," continued Ponzi. "These aren't bad people. They should get a fair shake — a decent rate of return for their hard-earned savings — and I'm giving it to them. They deserve to get ahead if they can, don't you agree?"

"Yes, but how are you making your money?"

"Why don't you ask those bankers on the corner the same question? Why don't you ask those greedy scoundrels how much they are making with depositor's money and exactly how they are making it?"

"When they start paying fifty-percent interest in ninety days, you bet I will," said Edward.

"Fair enough. But its ironic isn't it? If I kept the money, no one would be interested in how much I made, or how little I paid. But if I give the money away, everyone is up in arms. The way the Securities Exchange Company makes money is very simple Mr. Dunn. Have you ever seen one of these?"

Ponzi produced an International Reply Coupon and handed it to Edward.

Lucy, meanwhile, was dealing with a crisis. A woman was standing at her desk sobbing while her husband glowered nearby.

"Please try to calm down and tell me what the problem is," Lucy suggested.

"Hubert, that's my husband there, he says we can't go home 'til I get my money back. See, I got this certificate yesterday and he says I'm a foolish woman. He says this is nothing but a criminal operation and I'll lose everything."

Lucy put her arm protectively around the woman and glowered back at the husband. "Don't worry. Your money is safe. I'm sure Mr. Ponzi will be able to help you."

Lucy knocked on the door to Ponzi's office where he still was meeting with Edward Dunn. "I'm sorry Mr. Ponzi, but there's a woman crying. Her husband says she has to get her money back."

Ponzi turned to his guest. "I hope you don't mind. This will only take a moment."

The wife and husband entered.

"I understand you'd like to cancel your certificate?" Ponzi asked the crying woman.

"I want my money back. My husband thinks you're nothing but a crook."

"Your husband is entitled to his opinion, as misinformed as it may be. However, you'll be happy to know that it is our policy to refund the full principal amount of your investment whenever you'd like it. This applies to all of our depositors. Of course, I'm sure you understand that it won't include the fifty-percent interest you'd earn if you left it until maturity."

"Let's see the certificate." The woman showed it to him. "That's one hundred dollars." Ponzi removed cash from his wallet and gave it to her. "Now if you'll just sign the certificate to show that you've been paid, that should take care of it."

The woman signed. "Thank you Mr. Ponzi." She turned to her husband. "See Hubert, I told you he was okay."

"Thank you sir." The humbled husband offered his hand and Ponzi shook it.

"I hope this will reassure your family and friends that they can have confidence doing business with the Securities Exchange Company." And the happy couple walked out the door.

"So, Mr. Dunn, that's how we do business. You'll have to forgive me now. I have matters to attend to, but you're welcome back anytime."

Ponzi stopped in front of Lucy's desk. "Miss Melli, thirty days after a customer has purchased a certificate, please send them a postcard that tells them we wish to share our tremendous success with them. So, we will be happy to pay the full amount of their certificate, with interest, after only forty-five days."

"So, soon?" asked Lucy.

"That's right. We'll give them more than they're expecting."

"Will do, Mr. Ponzi."

Chapter 17

Surprise!

Ponzi and Rose sat at the kitchen table eating breakfast and reading The Boston Post. There was an article on the third page with the headline "Company Promises Fifty Percent," and the byline was Edward Dunn's.

"This article is going to create quite a stir. I'll have to warn Miss Melli to be prepared for the crowds tomorrow," Ponzi tells his wife.

Rose looks anxious. "You promised Charles, no business on Sunday."

"Yes, dear," said Ponzi and looked at his watch. "It's time pussycat. Get your hat. Keep your eyes open and come with me. I don't want you to miss anything."

1918 Locomobile

The couple stepped outside to see a shiny new Locomobile town car sitting at the curb. Its length, complex chrome work and glossy enamel were enough for any ten cars. A uniformed driver opened the rear door for them. Rose is stunned.

"Go on Rose, get in. It's ours."

"Really?"

"Yes, really."

Rose entered the vehicle but was afraid to touch anything. "It must've cost a fortune," she marveled.

"I'm making a fortune. Why not spend it?"

"Where are we going?" she asked in wonder.

"It's a surprise," grinned Ponzi, thinking of what a big surprise it truly was.

The Locomobile motored all the way to the posh community of Lexington and pulled in front of a grand house and the driver got out to open the passenger door.

"Are we visiting someone?" Rose asked as she timidly stepped out of the automobile.

"We are visiting ourselves," Ponzi replied. "This is your new home."

"My home? Oh Charles. I don't know what to say."

Ponzi's House in Lexington

"Isn't it beautiful? It has twenty rooms. I think you'll be so happy here, with mother of course."

"Mother? My mother? Oh, your mother. You could have told me you know."

"I wanted to surprise you."

"I am surprised. But, I'm not ready for her." Rose grew concerned.

"Yes, you'll need to buy furniture and take measurements for curtains and such. The store can help you find what you need and you can spend like a queen."

Chapter 18

More Surprises

Ponzi was glad to be back at the office when Monday finally rolled around. The main office was full of customers as it usually was now, all different kinds of people.

Ponzi was on the phone doing a little sideline business "...Yes, I understand," he said. "You don't want to sell your shares in the Hanover.... I'm not asking you to sell them. They'd be of no use to me. But, Mr. Menotti, if you are willing to form a coalition with several other stockholders — Mr. Constanza, Mr. Fasco, Mr. Locatelli and me— that will give us real power and no one has to sell a thing."

Lucy opened the office door.

"Just a moment," he told the caller and covered the mouthpiece and looked at Lucy for an explanation.

"Sorry, but there's a man here who says he has to see you right away. His name is Cassullo."

Ponzi looks stricken. "A skinny guy with bad skin?"

"He's standing next to my desk," said Lucy.

Ponzi half stood and looked into the main office. Cassullo, dressed in a suit, indeed was waiting there. Ponzi immediately sat down.

"Tell him I'm busy... Tell him I can't see him... Tell him to come back tomorrow... No, wait, tell him to go to The Bell in Hand and I'll be there in twenty minutes."

Lucy left to complete her mission and Ponzi took a deep breath and resumed his phone conversation.

"Sorry about that. An old friend stopped by. Now where was I? Right. So, will you join our little group of Hanover stockholders?" he asked.

"Good, I thought you would."

Ponzi walked in the door of The Bell in Hand and found Cassullo sitting at the bar tossing back a shot.

A Dubious Character

"There ya be old friend. I was thinkin' maybe you stood me up. Cassullo spoke with a tinge of an accent. Perhaps it was Irish or French Canadian. He stood and moved to embrace Ponzi who backed up a step.

"Let's go to the back where it's quiet," suggested Ponzi.

Diane and Amy Newly were also sitting at the bar while Amy took a break from her job. Diane stared at Ponzi.

"That's that guy Ponzi," she whispered to Amy.

"Who is Ponzi?" asked Amy.

"That guy I told you about, the one who pays all the money."

"The one who's paying fifty percent in ninety days?" Amy asked. "That can't be legal."

"He just sent me a postcard telling me that I don't need to wait ninety days for my money. I'm getting it in a couple of weeks. All of it."

"Really?" Amy asked.

"Yes. I told you. He's okay."

"Yeah, but did you see the weasel he was with?" asked Amy.

"So, miss my point," Diane said, annoyed that her sister hadn't been interested in investing too.

Ponzi chose a small table in the otherwise unoccupied back room and took a seat.

"I saw you was in the paper," said Cassullo. That's quite an operation you've got going, ya lucky bastard. Me? I've had my ups and downs. Downs mostly. But you're sitting pretty."

"If you're looking for a job…" Ponzi started

"What's the racket? Cassullo cut Ponzi off. "Can ya cut me in?"

Ponzi responded with growing alarm. "The Securities Exchange Company is a legitimate business."

"Right. Okay. So tell me about a job."

"No promises," said Ponzi. "We'll try something and see how it works out."

"What you thinkin'?" Cassullo pressed.

"I get calls from people that want to open branch offices. I need someone to check the people out, take a look at their operation, get them set up. You'd travel but you'd have a car, a salary, and your hotel and food would be paid."

"Do I get a piece of the action?"

"It's salary plus travel expenses. But if you come up with people who'll put cash up front for a branch office we can cut you in for a piece. But every thing's got to be on the up and up," Ponzi stressed.

"I got it boss."

"Don't call me boss, and don't hang around the office. You only deal with me. Understand? Call me on the telephone and I'll tell you who to see."

"Sounds good."

Chapter 19

Big Business

Each day the crowd at the Securities Exchange Company grew larger. The postcards that Lucy sent every customer after thirty days promising to reward them with their full interest in only forty-five days seemed to be working.

A short woman was beaming like she'd just won the lottery when she got to the front of the line she'd been waiting in. When it was finally her turn she stepped up to the teller and handed him the postcard.

"I got this in the mail," she said.

"Just sign the certificate and I'll give you your money," the teller told her.

The woman signed with the pen attached to the counter.

"Here's your ten dollars, plus one, two, three, four, five dollars in interest."

The woman left the cash on the counter and reached into her purse for more.

"I just wanted to see if you were really going to pay me. Now give me one of those for a hunerd and fifty."

On the way out of the office, and down the stairs, the woman announced to those waiting in line, "I got my money. Got all of it, and fifty-percent interest too. I hope there's some left for you."

The line of people waiting to get into the main office to hand over their hard earned money extended from the door and snaked around the corner to Pi Alley. There were two policemen now keeping order, but there was a feeling of elation in the air and when Ponzi's Locomobile pulled up to the curb, and the driver got out and opened the door for Ponzi who tipped his hat to the cheering crowd it was as if a celebrity had just arrived and the crowd began to cheer.

The flower seller handed Ponzi a red carnation that he tucked into his lapel, but now he had buckets of red carnations, and many of the young men who dreamed of riches of their own someday were sporting red carnations in their own lapels. Ponzi shook hands with some of the more fortunate people in line, bantered with the young women and patted children on the head.

Soon the line of people snaked all the way to the end of the alley, yet the wait didn't seem to discourage people. Why on the contrary. It was as if Mr. Ponzi had invited everyone to the best party in town.

Even a disabled veteran who was missing a leg and hobbling on crutches was enjoying the spectacle. "I'm a lucky man," he told his line mates. "I survived the Great War to see this."

A catholic priest explained to those nearby that he'd come to help the poor orphans of the flu epidemic that had devastated young adults just months before.

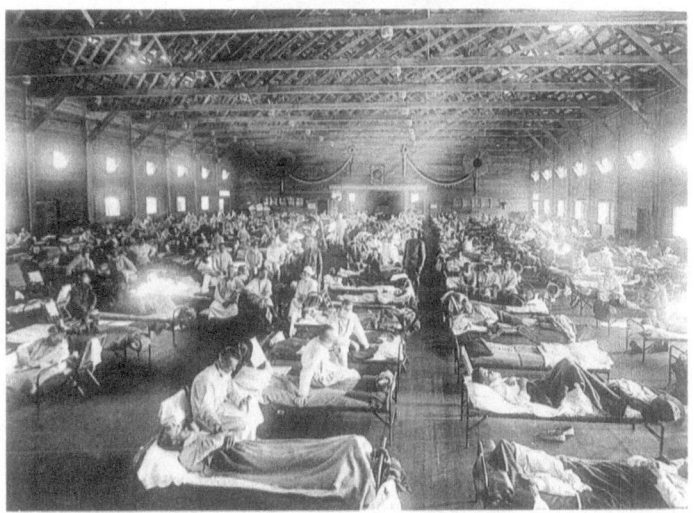

Flu Epidemic of 1918

A widow dressed in black with a hundred dollars in her pocket came because her husband had died and his pension had ended. "What else can I do?" she wondered.

At the very far end of the line of people waiting to give Mr. Ponzi money was The Bell in Hand with a "Closed" sign on the door and a "For Rent" sign in the window. Prohibition had officially begun and the only people who were happy about that were members of the Women's Temperance Union and teetotalers.

Temperance Activist Carrie Nation

Chapter 20

How Rude

Richard Grozier was still occupying the Publisher's office where he was having a "meeting" with Edward Dunn. Sadly, their meeting had been interrupted by a call from Richard's mother who was still summering on Cape Cod.

"Yes mother, but is this really necessary?" he asked. After a long pause, during which he was browbeaten in various motherly ways, he told her, "I'll see what I can do."

Richard covered the phone and spoke to Edward. "It's a social emergency. There's a shortage of bachelors for Mrs. Kennedy's party this weekend. Mother wants me to invite someone.... Wait, you're a bachelor."

"Don't worry Mother. I think I've found someone to endure this event with me."

Richard continued to listen to his mother's rant and rolled his eyes.

"It's black tie? Seriously? I look like a penguin in a tuxedo."

When Richard got off the phone, he thanked Edward for his "help." "It shouldn't be too bad really," he assured him. "Emergency handled. So, what's on the agenda now?" he asked.

"I'm going to need a photographer for the Ponzi story on Sunday."

"Ponzi? That little Italian again? Hasn't he been caught yet?"

"I don't know if he's a crook or not, but readers love his get-rich-quick story. I'm interviewing him at his pricey new house in Lexington."

"The guy is a con." Richard accused. "He must be."

"So far everything seems on the up and up. No complaints. No police record," Edward explained.

"You always were a sucker for a self-made man."

"Hey! Just because I wasn't born with a silver spoon in my mouth."

"I'm just saying watch out for this fellow Ponzi," Richard warned. "We don't need egg on our face."

"Don't worry. I've got investigators working with me."

And indeed he did, for just about at the same time, three large men in uniform, marched down School Street in a wedge.

The flower seller extended a red carnation. "A carnation like Mr. Ponzi's?" he asked.

"Step aside," the biggest of the three men ordered, and they tramped up the stairs, jostling the people waiting in line as they went.

"Move it!" they ordered. "Police comin' through."

After barging into the main office, the three men blew right past Lucy to where Ponzi stood with Rose and Uncle John.

"Are you Charles Ponzi?" one of them blurted out rudely. And when Ponzi confirmed that he was, he was told, "We need to talk."

Rose and Uncle John appeared to be very distressed. But Ponzi politely told the three men. "Please have a seat in my office. I'll be with you in a moment," and the threesome filed into Ponzi's office.

"This may take a while," Ponzi explained to Uncle John. "Will you wait with Rose?"

"What's happening Charles?" a worried Rose asked. "Are you in some sort of trouble?"

"Everything's fine," he told her and asked her to wait.

Chapter 21

The

American Way

"Gentlemen, who are you and why did you come barging in here frightening my poor wife like that?" asked Ponzi, who took a seat at his desk.

"I'm Mosby, Chief Inspector Police Department and this is my boss, Police Commissioner Curtis."

"Inspector Brown with the US Postal Service," said the third

"People have been asking a lot of questions about you and we're here to get answers."

Boston Police Officials

"I expect people to talk about me, but I don't appreciate your intimidation tactics. If you have a warrant, show it. Otherwise, leave or, if you prefer, stay as my guests. Care for a cigar? Or would that be considered a bribe?"

Ponzi opened the humidor on his desk, and after each "guest" took a cigar, he took one himself.

"We understand that you're speculating in International Reply Coupons. How are you getting them in such large quantities — unless of course, you're printing them?" asked Brown.

"Surely you'd be aware of any counterfeit coupons. Have you had any complaints?"

"Look, I'm not sure what your racket is, but we intend to find out. If you're making so much money, how much are the taxpayers losing?" asked the Commissioner. "I say it looks like you're taking it from the government."

Ponzi stood and paced as he spoke quickly, gesturing with his cigar for emphasis.

"The government losing money? Not a single wretched penny. I'm sure you are aware that International Reply Coupons are commodities — like postage stamps. They are sold by the postal service, which, being a government monopoly, the government guarantees regardless of whether it shows a profit or a deficit. In 1907, the International Postal Congress of Rome formed the Universal Postal Union. No member country can refuse to sell me stamps. The government can't even limit the number of coupons I can buy. If the demand is there, they must increase the supply. In other words, the burden of living up to the agreement is entirely the government's, not mine. All I have to do is pay cash for the coupons I want, all that I want. The government must exchange coupons for stamps. What I do with the stamps is my own business. There is no law, rule, or regulation I can possibly violate. In fact, the laws protect me and not the various governments concerned. And gentlemen, since you are government officials, it is your job to uphold my rights in this matter. After all, this is America."

"Hear, hear," said Curtis, and that seemed to put a cherry on top.

"Now gentlemen, I'd like to get back to my wife. We are expecting an important visitor today."

The officials stood and shook Ponzi's hand before he returned to his wife. "See, that wasn't so bad. Give me a smile. Let's forget this business and have some fun."

Chapter 22

Taking the Plunge

The beautiful stretched Locomobile sat at the curb with the driver at the ready. When Ponzi, Rose, and Uncle John left the Niles Building and climbed into the spacious backseats they were giddy with all the attention. They laughed and waved at the cheering crowds through the open windows and smiled for the photographers. Rose waved to the gawkers as they drove past them all the way to the railroad station.

Ponzi, Rose, and Uncle John were standing on the platform waiting when the train pulled into the station right on time. When Imelda Ponzi appeared at the top of the stairs in the first passenger car, Ponzi yelled with uncharacteristic enthusiasm. "There she is! Here I am Mother! Look this way!"

The white-haired Imelda, still wearing a widow's black dress, was imperial and stone-faced. Ponzi helped her down the stairs and she gave him a stiff embrace.

"You never write to me. You think I was dead?"

Imelda looked critically at her surroundings.

"Mother, this is my wife Rose and her Uncle John."

"Welcome mother. I'm so glad you're here." Rose moved to embrace her mother-in-law, but Imelda extended a formal gloved hand as she approached and simply stared at Uncle John as if he were a non-human specimen.

Ponzi, Imelda, Rose and Uncle John rode silently home in the Locomobile. Imelda had the ability to suck the joy right out of the air.

The following day, Ponzi, Rose and Imelda, dressed impeccably in their brand new clothing, posed for the photographer who came with Edward Dunn for his article about them that would be published in The Boston Post. First, all three of them posed together, then Ponzi alone, then with his mother, and finally, a shy Rose.

Rose, Charles & Imelda Ponzi

"You certainly have a lovely wife Mr. Ponzi," complimented Edward.

"She's everything to me Mr. Dunn. Everything. Now if you'll excuse me."

Diane and Amy Newly arrived at the Securities Exchange Company offices well before opening time to avoid the crowds, but it still took more than an hour before they were standing in front of a teller.

"Oh lord, I'm so nervous. Are you sure this is all right?" Amy asked her sister.

"Let's see, the bank was paying you four percent per year, and this company will pay you four-hundred percent per year. Seems to me you'd be crazy not to."

"You promise?" asked Amy.

"Promise," Diane replied. "But what do you have to worry about? You'll be teaching with me soon. This is just extra money."

"Next," the teller called out.

Amy stepped to the window and counted out her cash. "I'd like to purchase a five-hundred dollar certificate."

The teller completed the certificate, filling out the necessary details. "Just bring it back in ninety days and we'll give you seven hundred and fifty dollars. Next."

Amy took the certificate and Diane stepped to the window.

"I got this postcard in the mail and here's my certificate. I'd like to cash it in," Diane told the teller.

"Just sign the back," he instructed and counted out nine hundred dollars into Diane's open hand.

Lucy Melli walked behind the teller's windows with a wastebasket half-full of cash.

Line at the Securities Exchange Company

"Can I take some cash off your hands?" she asked the teller.

"Oh, good. I was running out of places to put it." The teller opened an over-flowing cash drawer, grabbing stacks of bills, and threw them into the wastebasket. Lucy made a move to walk away. "Wait. There's more." The teller crouched down to get piles of cash stacked on the floor and added them to the wastebasket.

Ponzi was at his desk when Lucy entered with the wastebasket full of cash. "We must be at nearly ten thousand today."

"More than that," Lucy replied. "Look, there's another basket hidden in the corner."

"And how many branches do we have now?" he asked.

"We added our twenty-sixth yesterday."

"Look here in The Boston Post. It's a photo of Rose, Mother and me and the new house."

The furniture seller Daniel's face appeared in the window of Ponzi's office, nose to the glass. He made no effort to draw Ponzi's attention.

"I'll send guards to take you to the bank," Ponzi offered and left the office.

"Visiting your old furniture Daniels?" Ponzi asked as he breezed past Daniels, not waiting for his response.

"Just checking how my old partner Mr. Ponzi is doing," said Daniels to no one. "Looks like pretty good."

Chapter 23

Returns

There are times when it was entirely an honor to bestow the Boston Post Cane upon a venerable citizen of Boston, and this was just such an occasion. Richard Grozier stood next to an ancient veteran dressed in a Union Civil War uniform. The room was packed with his family members, eager to be a part of this historic moment, including at least twenty overdressed grand and great-grandchildren. The photographer was on hand for this elevated moment.

Richard began his speech. "On behalf of all of us with the Boston Post, we are thrilled and delighted to honor you today, on the occasion of your 100th birthday. I'm sure that your children and many grandchildren and great-grandchildren will join me in congratulating you. And, as a small token of our regard, we'd like to bestow upon you an official Boston Post Cane.

As Richard picked up the cane and formally extended it to him, the old man grew rigid and backed away.

"Oh dear. Are you all right Mr. Kelly?" Richard approached the obviously distressed man.

"Back off now spawn of death," the old man yelled.

"Wha?" Richard looked around seeking the source of the old man's distress.

"Get that damn thing away from me," the venerable veteran warned loudly.

Civil War Veteran

"But, Mr. Kelly, it's nothing but a cane. A simple walking cane!" Richard explained.

"Don't listen to him! That thing is cursed!"

"It is?" asked the perplexed Richard as he examined the cane.

"Don't you know what happens to people who take that cane?" the vet continued to yell.

"What? What?" Richard yelled back in alarm.

"THEY DIE!"

"AAAAAAAAAAAAh!" screamed the children. "Don't die grandpa!"

A group of frightened children surrounded Richard and pummeled him with their fists.

"Don't hurt our grandpa!"

Bedlam ensued as children screamed and rushed to protect their grandfather, or sought the shelter of a parent's arms.

Entirely unexpected, Richard's father, Edwin Grozier opened the door and stepped into the room. "What's going on in here?" he demanded, but he was quickly interrupted by a group of children who threatened to overwhelm him as they rushed the door to escape.

"Richard, you're an idiot!" the elder Grozier fumed. It's worse than I could possibly have imagined. I must have been crazy to think you could run a newspaper. You're so incompetent you can't even give things away."

But, Edwin Grozier was not the only important arrival that day.

Main Floor, Boston Bank

The staff at the Hanover Bank was all smiles, opening doors and warm greetings when Mr. Charles Ponzi arrived. The receptionist in the president's office met him at the entrance to the inner sanctum. "Mr. Chmielinski is expecting you," she told Ponzi as she pulled the massive door open for him.

Mr. Chmielinski, the bank president, offered his hand. Ponzi ignored it. "Good day Mr. Ponzi. How may we help you? Please have a seat."

Chmielinski indicated one of the chairs in front of his desk with a gesture of welcome.

"I see you've been reading the papers," Ponzi sneered as he took the seat.

"I try to keep up on things. You've been quite a news item these days," Chmielinski acknowledged from behind his desk.

"Let's stop the chit chat. I've come to buy stock in the bank."

"I'm sorry Mr. Ponzi. I'm afraid all the shares in the Hanover have been spoken for."

"That's not what I've heard. I understand that your Board of Director's has approved a new issue for two thousand shares and I'd like you to sell them all to me."

Chmielinski laughed. "Why Mr. Ponzi, that would give you control of the bank. I'm sure you'll understand. I couldn't possibly do that — certainly not without approval from the Board of Directors."

Ponzi pulled a checkbook from his pocket and wrote.

"Then I'm certain you'll understand why I'm doing this. I'd hate to be the one to explain to your Board of Directors why I withdrew all my money. Can you tell me what my balance is?"

Charles Ponzi

"You're planning to withdraw your entire balance?" asked the now serious bank president.

"Certainly. Right now. In cash. What's my balance?" Ponzi asked again.

"One moment please." Chmielinski picked up the phone and prepared to write.

"Chmielinski here," he announced into the phone. "I need the current balance on the account of Mr. Charles Ponzi. Yes, the full amount."

The two men waited wordlessly while some bookkeeper found the account and reported back to the president.

"What? Are you certain?" Chmielinski looked stricken and slammed down the phone.

"Mr. Ponzi, you have nearly a half a million dollars in your account!"

"This is hardly news to me," replied Ponzi.

"But, so much money, on such short notice? The bank closes in ten minutes!"

"Is there a problem? My money is in a checking account. Is there any reason I shouldn't write a check to the full extent of my balance?"

"But a bank doesn't keep such large amounts of cash on hand. In order to honor your check we have to sell securities, probably at a loss," explained the now worried Chmielinski.

"That does not concern me. On the other hand, what if word of this gets out to your depositors? They'd want to take their money out at once. It could start a run on the bank!" Ponzi pointed out.

"That would be terrible!"

"Yes, for you it would be. On the other hand, most of your depositors would probably just take their cash across the street and invest with my company," smiled Ponzi.

"Mr. Ponzi, can't we compromise?"

"What do you have to offer me?" Ponzi asked.

"We'll sell you one thousand shares of the new stock," offered Chmielinski, daubing the sweat from his brow with his handkerchief.

"Doesn't interest me," Ponzi yawned. "Sorry, we can't get together on that basis."

"But Mr. Ponzi, the bank only controls fifteen-hundred shares," the trapped man pled.

"Then sell me fifteen-hundred shares and agree to make me a director.

"What choice do I have?"

"Beats me," Ponzi shrugged.

Meanwhile, not everything was peaches and cream in Ponzi's life. His home in Lexington had become a tourist attraction. All day long a string of cars trolled slowly by, the passengers eager to see family members who were now often sequestered inside.

People were so curious about the now famous man and his family that they would park, get out of their cars and wander around the house or take pictures of their own family standing and smiling for the camera out on the manicured lawn. This made the Ponzi family unpopular with the neighbors.

If someone did step out of Ponzi's house, perhaps onto the veranda, the tourists would just stand there like they were looking at zoo animals, commenting on them out loud, taking pictures.

"Look! That must be his mother come all the way from Italy!"

"HELLO!" the tourists yelled and waved cheerfully at whomever they saw.

"Go away crazy Americans," Imelda would respond with visible disgust. (She was learning English.)

It didn't take long for the bank clerks to prepare the stock certificates for Mr. Ponzi, and when they were ready the receptionist handed the certificates to Chmielinski, who handed them to Ponzi.

"I assume you'll find those satisfactory," said the exhausted bank president.

Ponzi examined the certificates.

"Just one more thing," said Ponzi. "You see, I also have in my possession proxies from several of the Hanover's other stockholders. Altogether they total six hundred shares. Combined with those you've just sold me, I now have controlling interest in the Hanover Bank."

"No! That can't be. Oh my God!" Chmielinski clutched his heart.

"I'm not your god Mr. Chmielinski. I'm your boss... "

"My boss?"

"That's right. You report to me now. And if you want to keep your job, you'll do just as I tell you to."

Chmielinski was aghast.

"Let's see. Where shall I begin? For starters, I've taken a fancy to your office. You see my office in the Niles Building has become rather noisy and I need a nice quiet place to think. This place should fill the bill. Please find another office and move there immediately."

Chapter 24

The Big Night

Brookline was a neighborhood of up and comers like young Boston banker, Joseph P. Kennedy Sr. and his wife Rose Kennedy, and their business associates and friends. Although this lovely suburban neighborhood was typically subdued, it was clear that something special was going on in the Kennedy household that night. All the chandeliers were shining through sparkling windows and the service staff was bustling about.

Two small boys, Joseph Jr, age four and John, age two, both in pajamas were running around, giggling, as their father attempted to corral them to get them to go to bed. Their nanny stood nearby holding a tiny baby.

Joseph Kennedy Sr. with Sons Joseph Jr. & John F.

"Come on John. You too, Joe. It's time for bed boys. Let's go upstairs and tuck you in," suggested dad.

"We want Mamma to tuck us in," demanded Joseph Jr.

"Mamma!" echoed little John.

"Mamma's busy getting ready for a party," senior explained.

"I wanna go to the party!" said the excited four-year-old.

"Party!" his little brother parroted.

Joseph Sr., realizing that he'd made an error talking about the party, said, "Not tonight boys. This party is for daddy's banker friends. You know how boring they can be."

"Boring!" they both agreed. "But can we have cake?" asked the elder.

"We'll save you some for tomorrow. Who'll be the first one in bed?" asked Sr.

"I will!" yelled Jr. and they both scampered up the stairs.

Soon after, the party had begun in earnest as a group of beautifully dressed guest, both bankers and dignitaries, including the French Ambassador Jusserand and his wife, on their first assignment to the US since the big war. Everyone was seated at the long table covered in white linens and set with porcelain, crystal and silver.

Some of the uniformed servers brought carts of steaming dishes from the kitchen where they'd been prepared by the cooking staff, overseen by a well-known chef, and offered the savory dishes at the left elbow of each guest. Others were pouring wine, all imported from France for their guests of honor.

Richard Grozier and Edward Dunn were also present, dressed in tuxedos, and seated next to the ladies they were to entertain.

Gentlemen in Top Hats

At the end of the meal, Kennedy Sr. drew the attention of his guests. "Mr. and Mrs. Ambassador, I think Mrs. Kennedy has planned a little surprise for you."

A maid rolled in a cake decorated with the French flag and candles. "We didn't want the two of you to celebrate Bastille Day alone," said Mrs. Kennedy.

"Merci! Merci!" exclaimed the ambassador.

"How do you celebrate Bastille Day in France?" asked one of the banker's wives.

"We drink champagne, and sing." In order to prove his point, the Ambassador stood and belted out a verse.

"Allons enfants de la patrie,
Le jour de gloire est arrivé!
Contre nous, de la tyrannie
L'étendard sanglant est levé..."

Everyone cheered and the champagne corks began to pop and glasses were filled. Kennedy lifted his glass. "To France. Quickly may she recover and long may she stand."

Everyone lifted their glass and responded, "Long live France."

Mrs. Kennedy also lifted her glass to toast the honored guests. "Well, I'd say let them eat cake, but you know what happened the last time someone said that."

The event in Brookline wasn't the only thing going on in Boston that night. The Plymouth Theater was crowded with people. A spotlight illuminated the organist who added musical pathos and drama as a silent black-and-white newsreel was shown.

First the audience learned that Jack Dempsey, had been crowned the new heavyweight champion of the world. The viewers were treated to the highlights of the fight, and the last moments of the final round ending with the referee lifting Dempsey's gloved hand.

Then, in a moment of civic pride, the seated Bostonians discovered that one of their own had made the national news, and so they spontaneously cheered when a strutting Charles Ponzi appeared on screen, twirling his cane. The on-screen caption read: "Financial wizard, Charles Ponzi takes Boston by storm."

Charles Ponzi

Next, scenes of the lines of people in Pi Alley fill the screen. Many smiled and waved at the camera. "Customers of Ponzi's Securities

Exchange Company wait in line to earn 50% interest," read the caption.

Then the audience was treated to film of the Locomobile pulling up in front of the house in Lexington. The driver opened the car door and Ponzi exited. Rose ran down the stairs, smiled and waved for the camera and greeted Ponzi with a hug. The caption was, "Ponzi and his wife Rose are enjoying their millions."

The newsreel ended, the organist played a fanfare and the spot light was turned on the audience to find Ponzi himself sitting in the first balcony with Rose. The audience cheered uproariously. Ponzi stood and bowed.

Chapter 25

Party Night

The gentlemen at the Kennedy party had retired to the salon to smoke cigars and drink brandy after the meal, and, of course, perhaps talk a little business if the topic should come up.

It was obvious that Joe Kennedy was eager to score points with the French Ambassador. "We lost a lot of good men during the war Mr. Ambassador, but nothing like the disaster you folks had. Rebuilding Europe is our top priority, and we want you to know that Boston's banks are behind you."

There was a murmur of general agreement and a few words of appreciation from the Ambassador.

One of the bankers held a snifter to the light to admire the golden color of its contents. "Glad to see Prohibition hasn't changed the quality of your cognac, Joe."

"And it never will," smiled Kennedy. "Not if I have anything to do with it."

"First Prohibition, and now we have this Ponzi character to deal with," said the banker looking genuinely worried.

"A dreadful little man," asserted another banker.

"A complete scoundrel if you ask me," added yet another.

"Edward here has met him, spoken with him," offered Richard Grozier.

"Oh really?" came the coldly surprised reaction from one of the guests. "Do tell us Edward, what do you think of Charles Ponzi?"

Edward took a breath. "He's very persuasive and what he is doing looks suspicious to everyone, but so far, the Police Commissioner and the Chief Inspector haven't been able to hang anything on him. Even the Postal Inspector can't poke holes in him."

"How persuasive do you have to be when you're giving money away?" Kennedy pointed out. "I don't know about your bank, but our small depositors are leaving in droves. How do you convince someone that it's better to earn a safe four percent when Ponzi says he'll give you four hundred?"

"You can't," agreed one of the others. "And at those rates, can our large depositors be far behind?"

"Yes, it's worrisome," said another, "but what can we do?"

"Simple," asserted Kennedy. "You prove the business is a scam, which it is."

"But how do we do that? How do we prove it to our depositors?"

"There's only one thing I know that will reliably strike terror in the heart of any red-blooded American finance man — honest or not."

"What's that Joe?"

"An audit!" said Kennedy.

Everyone gasped at the utter horror that word evoked, and the doorbell rang. Mrs. Kennedy appeared soon after. "Our entertainment has arrived. Would you gentlemen join us in the parlor?"

While leaving the salon after everyone else, Edward discovered Amy and Diane Newly and Eduardo dressed for performance, standing by the door to the parlor waiting for their cue. Edward recognized Amy. "You're the girl from The Bell in Hand aren't you?"

"I remember you!" Amy replied with surprise.

"Small world. What are you doing here?" he whispered.

"Shhhh!" Diane scolded.

"Can't talk now," Amy said.

In the parlor, the guests were sitting and standing in a circle around the room. Richard stood behind a seated Edward. A bandoneón player sat by the door holding his instrument at the ready.

Mrs. Kennedy took the floor in the now clear center of the room and addressed her guests. "I hear that all of Paris is in love with a new dance called the Tango. As a surprise we've invited the Newly sisters, Amy and Diane, to perform the Tango for us with the help of Eduardo from Argentina."

Eduardo entered with a sister on each arm to a smattering of applause as the bandoneón began.

Richard, in an aside to Edward asked, "Do all tango dancers get two women?"

Eduardo and Diane danced a slow, sensuous duet that completed with a flourish. The Ambassador and his wife gave enthusiastic bravos and the dancers took a bow.

"Encore. Encore," demanded the Ambassador.

Tango Dancers

This time Eduardo led Amy to the center of the floor. The music began, but a few moments into the dance, Amy's heel broke and she fell into an astonished Edward's lap.

"Does this mean that Edward gets to keep her?" asked Richard.

Everyone laughed at the joke, but Edward was genuinely concerned. "Are you okay?" he asked the lovely in his lap.

"I think I've hurt my ankle," she replied.

"Let's see if you can stand on it," suggested Edward.

Richard and Diane helped Amy to her feet and then Edward suggested she lean on him. Amy winced.

"Let's go put some ice on it," offered Edward like a good knight.

Edward and Amy went to the kitchen where Amy was carefully lowered onto a chair. Edward knelt at her feet with her foot in his hands. Gently he rotated her ankle. A maid chipped small pieces of ice from a huge block into a basin. "Fortunately, I don't think it's broken," he told her.

"I'm glad to hear that," said the much-relieved Amy.

"You'll need to stay off it for a while, but it should be fine in a few weeks," doctor Edward told the patient.

"A few weeks?" responded the patient. "What about dancing? I teach Tango for a living now."

"So that's what you've been doing. I wondered what happened to you. I'm sorry, I'm afraid you won't be dancing for a while."

"This is terrible," and she broke down in tears.

"I'm sorry," Edward told her again.

"It's not your fault" Amy sniffed.

Chapter 26

Opportunists

It was completely dark when the phone rang. Edward Dunn struggled to pull his consciousness back from dreamland to discover what was making that dreadful sound. He found the receiver and picked it up.

"Hello?"

A bedside lamp switched on and the alarm clock showed it was 4:32 AM.

"What've you got?" he asked. Suddenly Edward straightened with interest and scratched notes on the back of an envelope. "Holy mackerel. Okay, I'm on it," he told the caller and hung up the phone.

The sun was rising by the time the taxi got to Ponzi's house in Lexington. Edward stepped out of a cab, climbed the stairs and rang the bell. When no one answered, he pounded on the door.

Finally, Ponzi stepped out on the second floor porch in his dressing gown and yelled down to the intruder who was creating the ruckus.

"What the hell are you doing disturbing my peace at this ungodly hour? Go away or I'll call the police," Ponzi threatened.

"It's Dunn here with the Post, Mr. Ponzi. I just heard a story about you. I'd like to confirm it."

"I'll be right down."

Edward and Ponzi sat at the table in the huge dining room where the maid, still in her dressing gown, brought them coffee.

"A man named Daniels is suing you for a million dollars," Edward began. He claims he's your partner, that he loaned you the money to start your business."

"Daniels? The furniture seller?" asked Ponzi, incredulous. "That's really rich. Well, for the record, I did no such thing. I have no partners and my only dealing with that unpleasant man was to buy furniture from him — very bad furniture — make a note of that."

"He's represented by a top-notch law firm Mr. Ponzi. They say he's got the documents to prove it."

Furniture Seller

"His suit has no merit. Mr. Daniels had better pay his lawyers well because they'll get nothing from me."

"Then you aren't concerned about how your investors will take this news?" a slightly disappointed Edward asked, feeling that his story of the century might amount to little more that second page news.

"Concerned? No Mr. Dunn. The Securities Exchange Company has a history of dealing fairly with our investors. No one has ever lost a penny. While a million dollars may seem like a lot of money to most people, to me it is only a small percentage of the funds I control. Even if Mr. Daniels were to win his suit, which he won't, there would be no problem for our investors."

"Do you realize Mr. Ponzi, that Mr. Daniel's suit is blocking funds you hold in five different banks? Won't it be a problem if you can't access your money?"

"I have funds in over twenty banks. This is a mere nuisance. By the way, which five banks are those?" Mr. Ponzi was finally interested.

Young Child on Horseback

It was still early when the phone rang in the Chmielinski house. Sunday comics and toys were strewn about the oriental carpet and grandpa Chmielinski was on all fours entertaining his two cherubic grandchildren who were riding him like a horse.

"Giddy up horsie," ordered one grandchild. But when the phone rang the horsie reared a bit, threatening to dismount the pair, it was suddenly, "Whoa!"

"Grandpa has to answer the telephone now. You'll have to play without me," he explained and the children got off the horse.

"Hello.... Slow down please Mr. Ponzi. It's Sunday. I understand. You want to avoid having your funds frozen, but I can't do any banking business on Sunday.

Chmielinski continued to listen and winced. "Do you have to put it that way? I don't know. I'm thinking. Put the account in your wife's name? I guess that is too obvious. One moment."

Chmielinski fished for a pen and paper and wrote a name.

"Ready. Lucy Melli, M-E-L-L-I. Okay, I'll make the change as part of Saturday's business and submit it in the morning, but I have to wonder what you've gotten me into."

Chapter 27

Bad Press

It is early morning and the Securities Exchange Company is not yet open. The clock on the wall of the main office says 7:55. Lucy bustled as a guard snoozed in the corner. The tellers counted stacks of cash into their drawers. Customers in the hallway pushed against the door causing it to rattle. Lucy signaled them by holding up five fingers.

"Five minutes. We open in five minutes," she yelled.

She turned to the tellers. "My God. They are impatient today."

Suddenly there was the sound of breaking glass and a hand reached in to open the door. A flying wedge of people burst through the empty doorframe, then more flooded into the office, yelling that they wanted their money. The guard sprang into action. Lucy retreated to Ponzi's office and grabbed the phone.

"Police! Send the police!" she yelled into the phone "The second floor of the Niles Building. A mob has broken into our office."

Yells came from the street below drawing Lucy's attention. She looked out the window to see that intersection of School and Pi Alley was crammed with hundreds of people trying to get into the building. Policemen, nightsticks in hand, were attempting to maintain order.

Mob in Pi Alley

In near panic, Lucy dialed the phone again.

"Oh Lord, thank God you're there. You won't believe it Mr. Ponzi! The police are here. People broke in. There are thousands of them. The police said if we can't maintain order they'd close the place down!"

Ponzi was watching the action in the street from the window of his new office in the Hanover Bank building on the other side of School Street. "Don't worry," he told Lucy. "They're acting like beasts now, but once it dawns on people that I'm worth enough to sue for a million dollars — and they see we've got plenty of money to dish out — they'll be back demanding certificates in no time. Meanwhile stay calm. Just pay everyone who wants it. It's business as usual."

Actress Gabrielle Ray as St. Joan

"Stay calm. Pay everyone. Business as usual. Stay calm. Pay everyone. Business as usual," Lucy repeated to herself as she put on her game face. Then, there was the sound of more breaking glass. "Oh Lord," Lucy prayed, crossing herself, eyes skyward, hands clasping a rosary as if in prayer, she climbed up on a chair, and then to the top of a desk to address the throng.

"For the love of God, please listen. I've just spoken with Mr. Ponzi himself. He assures me that everyone will be paid. So form lines at the teller's windows and we'll process your paperwork as quickly as possible. You will all be paid."

Many in the room also crossed themselves and cheered.

As Ponzi stood at the window across the street looking down on the throngs that filled Pi Alley and flowed out onto School Street, he heard the crowds cheer as the good news that they'll be paid arrived after being passed from person to person.

Ponzi sat at his desk and unfolded the newspaper. An article blaring the headline "Ponzi Sued for a Million Dollars" was on the front page. Ponzi turned the paper over in disgust.

Below the fold another article appeared with the headline "U.S. to Sell 10,000 Retired Warships." He scanned the article, removed a pair of scissors from the drawer and cut it out, scribbled notes on a piece of paper and punched buttons on a calculator.

Chapter 28

Good Press

A taxi moved slowly through the human traffic at the corner of School and Pi Alley to the Hanover Bank and Richard Grozier stepped out.

There was a tap on the door of Ponzi's new office and then the receptionist opened the door a crack to announce. "Mr. Richard Grozier is here to see you sir."

"Aha! The vampire from that Boston Post is here for fresh blood."

Richard made an end run around the receptionist. "Sorry to intrude. I just need a moment Mr. Ponzi.

"Why the hell should I give you a moment of my time? Isn't this your work?" Ponzi asked, pointing to the newspaper.

"You can see for yourself, I had nothing to do with that article. Edward Dunn wrote it."

"But Dunn works for you doesn't he?"

"Not anymore," Richard answered.

"So you fired him? Good!" Ponzi smiled.

"Not exactly."

"He quit? The guessing game continued.

"No. no. Not that. Oh dear. I suppose you'll learn sooner or later."

"Learn what?" Ponzi asked, growing impatient.

"I'm no longer publisher for the Post. I don't even work there anymore."

"You quit then. Good, you're better off."

"I was fired. Terminated by the Chairman of the Board, Edwin Grozier," Richard confessed.

"Your own father fired you? My, that is a surprise. Why?"

"Because of you Mr. Ponzi. He said I'd missed the story of the decade — that you are the biggest thing to happen to Boston since the tea party."

"He said that?" Ponzi smiled and puffed up a bit.

"I was supposed to telegraph him if anything big was going on. Frankly, I didn't think you were such a big a deal."

"I think I've been insulted," Ponzi huffed.

"No offense intended. It's just your public image as a small-time operator, recent immigrant, and no school connections — you don't belong to a club. It just seemed like you weren't..."

"Now I know I've been insulted!"

"Don't worry. It's nothing that can't be fixed with the right public relations — you know, talking to the right editors, advertising in the right publications, donating to the right charities, being seen at the right events with the right people. It takes more than money to earn a reputation as a gentleman in Boston."

"I am very aware of that. Did you come to rub my nose in it? I know you're a blue blood while I'm merely exceedingly rich. What's your point?"

"I think you need me to counteract the bad press you've been getting — someone to fight your battles for you and win the public's praise. I'm just the man to do the job. I've got the background. I've got the connections. I think I can turn this around for you."

"But why would you do that?" asked a puzzled Ponzi.

"First, it would drive my father stark raving mad. I'd find an absurd sense of justice in that somehow. Then, there's all that lovely money."

"It is lovely, isn't it?"

Later that morning, across the street, Lucy was facing down the head of a line of people as they entered the door of the main office. One by one she greeted them.

"Good morning. How may I help you?"

"I want my money back. Now."

"No problem. Baby and mommy, to window number four."

Policewoman Directing Traffic

Salesman Jimmy Dupree arrived with a canvas bag. "Good morning Mr. Dupree. Mr. Waverly will process your deposit at window number two."

"Thanks Lucy," said Dupree, "Looks like you've got everything under control."

Cassullo was standing near the door with his canvas bag waiting for directions from Lucy and talking to Richard Grozier, the now new employee, who was also waiting to speak with her.

"Quite a tomato ain't she?" said Cassullo.

"Very attractive," Richard affirmed.

"If ya ask me, little Lucy there's got a "special" relationship with the boss if ya know what I mean." Cassullo guffawed.

Lucy responded immediately. "Mr. Cassullo, I heard that. Do I need to remind you again that I *am* the boss?"

"Riiiight. I forgot." Cassullo rolled his eyes.

"Take it to window five," Lucy instructed him.

"By the way Mr. Cassullo, after you're done there, I'd like to talk to you about the questionable certificates that continue to show up from your branches."

"Yeah, yeah, yeah."

Before heading to the window, Cassullo shared his opinion with Richard, "Americans must be crazy. First, they get rid of all the booze. Next thing ya know, they'll probly let women vote. Crazy people Americans. Even my 'ol pal Ponzi's getting to be a crazy American."

Cassullo continued to the window and now it was Richard's turn with Miss Melli at last. "May I help you sir?" asked Lucy politely."

Richard smiled warmly and asked. "If that man — Cassullo was it? If he isn't an American, I have to wonder which country kicked him out."

"Canada I think," responded Lucy.

"Wise decision on Canada's part. You must be Miss Melli. I'm Richard Grozier. Mr. Ponzi said I should see you."

"Right! He told me. You're the new public relations man. Come and I'll show you the office," and they both headed that way.

"I'm sorry," Lucy explained. "We'll have to share. It's our only office. But you can have the desk. I never get a chance to sit down anymore."

"Are you sure?" he asked.

"It's no problem. Just make yourself at home."

"Thank you. I'll be fine. By the way, it's nice to meet you. Boss."

Lucy smiled over her shoulder as she walked out the door.

Richard sat at the desk, opened a drawer full of office paraphernalia and closed it. Then he opened the file drawer. It was filled to the top with packets of hundred dollar bills.

"Dear Lord!"

He slammed it shut. Slowly he inched open the file drawer on the other side of the desk. It too was filled with cash.

Chapter 29

Pi Alley Circus

The storefront that used to be The Bell in Hand was no longer a bar. It was a construction site and soon to be the Annex for the Securities Exchange Company. Sawhorses, ladders, nail kegs and tools were scattered about. Carpenters were carrying lumber, hammering and sawing. A row of teller's cages stood where the bar once stood.

In the center of the room a group of nervous new tellers circled Lucy as a sign painter worked on a sign in the window

"This is going to be a busy day," warned Lucy.

"What if we run out of money?" asked one of the new tellers.

"That won't be a problem. You'll see that there are just as many people giving us money as there are people taking it away — maybe more," Lucy explained.

"What if we have to go to the bathroom?" asked another.

Outside the old bar, Amy Newly, leaning on a crutch, stood looking at the new sign reading "Securities Exchange Company Annex." She stood next to a matronly woman in a line of people snaking through Pi Alley.

"So this is what happened to the old place," Amy mused sadly.

"What old place?" the woman asked.

"This used to be The Bell in Hand. I was a barmaid here."

"I wish it was a bar now. I could use a drink."

"Why don't you get some of the coffee and donuts Ponzi is giving away? I'll hold your place."

"Can I bring you something?" the woman asked.

"No coffee for me," Amy replied. "I feel so hot."

"Suit yourself."

An organ grinder with his monkey played music to entertain the crowd. They watched as the monkey held his hat out to people in order to collect coins.

Organ Grinder with Monkey

"Look, it's Mr. Ponzi. He wants our money," laughed a young man still in knickers.

"But will he pay fifty percent in ninety days?" came a yell from the crowd.

"This Mr. Ponzi won't even give you back your penny."

A group of suffragettes carrying placards and collection cans slowly marched nearby chanting. "Votes for women! Votes for women!"

Suffragettes

Their leader, a woman with a megaphone, yelled, "Help us win the right to vote. Give us what you can. We only need seven more states. Please help us if you can."

And a chorus made up of all the other suffragettes chanted, "Help us win the right to vote. Put your pennies in the can," as they offered their collection cans to others in line.

The leader of the suffragettes held her can out for the monkey who dropped in a coin. "See, even a monkey knows that women should have the right to vote," she told the cheering crowd.

The Locomobile pulled up in front of the Niles Building and the driver rushed around to open the door for Ponzi who was quickly surrounded by reporters and photographers, including Edward Dunn.

The reporter for the Boston Globe told Ponzi, "The Boston Post says you're being sued for a million. A lot of depositors are worried."

"That's because a million dollars sounds like a lot of money to most folks. For me it's just small potatoes."

Another reporter asked, "Aren't you worried about what might happen if this man Daniels wins his lawsuit?"

Ponzi smiled and leaned casually against the car. He took cigars from his pocket and handed them out to the reporters. "Do I look concerned?" he asked. "You boys sound practically un-American."

"Some of our readers are concerned that you have might have loyalty to an Italian underworld operation. Any truth to that rumor Mr. Ponzi?"

"Not a bit of truth. What's more American than being a millionaire? I'm extremely proud of my Italian heritage. You know, Italians practically invented civilization as we know it. Columbus discovered America, Marconi discovered the wireless..."

"And Ponzi discovered money!" piped a paperboy. The crowd laughed.

A youth in knickers approached Ponzi. "Wow, what an honor. I'm so proud to meet you Mr. Ponzi. I'm a big believer. I don't care what they say. I think you're a true American. I hope I'm successful like you some day."

"What's your name son?" Ponzi asked.

"Robert Parker, sir."

"How'd you like to work for me Mr. Parker?"

"Are you serious? I'd love that sir."

Youth in Knickers

"Do you think you could round up a few more chaps who would like an opportunity to make some money?"

"Hell yes sir."

And so within a half hour, Robert Parker had gathered a handful of friends in the Annex and they were listening to Ponzi.

"Good day gentlemen. I'm going to give you a rare opportunity to make lots of money today. As a businessman, I must take advantage of any opportunity that lands in my lap, wouldn't you agree?"

Of course they would since they were taking advantage of an opportunity that had landed in their lap.

"Why should I pay full price for something I can buy at a discount?" asked Ponzi. "So, here's what I want you to do..."

Twenty minutes later Robert Parker was approaching people in line and asking, "Are you here to cash out your certificate?"

"Nope. I'm lookin' to buy."

"How bout you?" he asked the next person. "Are you here to cash out your certificate?"

"You bet."

"How long you been waiting?" Robert asked.

"Too long."

"Think you'll make it before they close?"

"I sure the hell hope I do."

"How 'bout I take that certificate off your hands, just buy it from you for cash?"

"You serious?"

"Sure am. How big is it?" asked Robert who was soon looking at a hundred-dollar certificate. "Give me a discount, say twenty percent. I'll give you cash and you can go home."

"Twenty percent? You must be crazy."

"Okay, I'm crazy. Is Ponzi's cash going to hold out long enough to pay everyone? I'll give you eighty dollars for it right now. You'll have most of your money back and you can go home."

"Deal."

Robert peeled four twenties off of a stack of bills.

"Hey, would you like to buy a thousand-dollar certificate?" asked the guy next to him.

"I'll give you eight hundred," offered Robert.

Chapter 30

Blow by Blow

Edward entered the main office of the Securities Exchange Company and ran into Richard Grozier coming out of the office he shared with Lucy.

"Good God, it's Richard Grozier. So it's true. You are working for this crook!"

"What about it?" Richard asked defensively.

"I hadn't really expected to find you here actually," Edward confessed.

"Look, let's cut to the chase. Since I left the Post, I needed a job."

"Left the Post? That's a bit of an understatement isn't it? Booted out might cover it better."

"Leave it to you to come up with a colorful take on the circumstances of my departure. In any case, yes, I'm employed by the Securities Exchange Company now."

"Doing what, pray tell?" Edward asked.

"Public relations."

Edward laughed. "You're a PR man for Charles Ponzi? You're serious? That's precious."

"This is where the action is," Richard claimed.

"Yes, if you call fleecing the public "action.""

"You don't know that for a fact do you? No one's holding a gun to anyone's head. Investors always put their money at risk."

"You think these are investors? Edward looked surprised. "The grandmother with the nickels she's been putting in the cookie jar for a rainy day for the last thirty years is an investor? An ironworker who's on strike for health benefits, hoping to stretch his last week's pay. That's your idea of an investor? These investors are widows whose husbands died in the flu epidemic leaving them a lousy grand in life insurance to bury him and raise six kids. Ponzi is taking money from file clerks who make less in a week than you spend on cigars. These are desperate people — the waiters and waitresses and bartenders whose jobs were wiped out by Prohibition. They're hoping to make the lousy tips you gave them feed their families until they can find another job. Meet the public, mister public relations man."

"Look, none of that's my fault..."

"Not your fault? You're helping this schmuck out and you don't think you have anything to do with stealing these people's money?"

"Do you have the goods on him Mr. Dunn? Do you know something I don't know? Look, if you know something..."

"Yeah I know something." Edward continued, getting angrier by the minute. "I know that there are a lot of people going to get hurt. He's a fraud. I haven't proved it yet but I will."

"Remember Mr. Dunn, this is Ponzi the self-made man. Weren't you Ponzi's big admirer?"

"Yeah, and I used to admire you too," spit a disappointed and angry Edward.

"I've got a tip for you..." says Richard.

"Keep it," says Edward who brought his fist back and slugged Richard in the jaw.

Richard looked entirely stunned but faked a return blow to the face, then slammed Edward in the gut.

Edward reeled backward, stripped off his jacket, and returned to the fray only to take a fist in the eye.

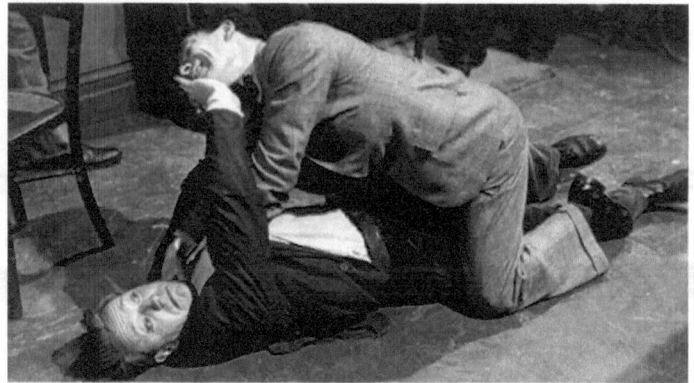

Brawlers

The two men wrestled each other to the floor with Richard, nose bleeding, finally grasping Edward in a headlock. Richard, panting, whispered. "You really are an idiot. I said I had a tip for you. I've got a lead for you to check out."

"Seriously?" said the now interested Edward, still under Richard's control.

"A man named Cassullo." Richard whispered. "He's a Canadian I think and he might be an old friend of Ponzi's."

"You've got a hunch about this guy?"

"That's right. A hunch." Richard released his captive.

Lucy ran up to the men. "Good Lord! Richard! Are you okay? Should I call the police?" She grabbed the handkerchief from his breast pocket and moved to daub his bleeding nose. "Poor baby," she said, all motherly affection.

"It's okay now. Due to my excellent public relations skills, Mr. Dunn promises to be a good boy."

Chapter 31

Feeling the Heat

The line of "investors" waiting in Pi Alley continued to grow despite the new tellers in the Annex. Amy Newly was exhausted, but like so many others, she continued to wait, standing for hour after hour with only the people near her, as desperate as she, for moral support.

"How much longer do you think it will be?" Amy asked the matronly woman, still next to her.

"Don't know. A couple more hours at least. Maybe longer." She looked around to assess the situation. "Probably longer."

"We've been here forever. It's so hot. I really need to sit down."

"No wonder. It's been over six hours," says her line mate.

"Oh god, I'm knackered," Amy complained.

Fresh from his battle with Richard, Edward walked by holding ice to his eye. He didn't see Amy.

"Mr. Dunn!" she yelled when she realized who it is. "What's happened to your eye?"

"Oh. Hello Amy. I'm sorry. I didn't see you. I'm blind on one side."

"Are you okay? Amy asked, all fluttery concern as she examined his battle wound.

"I had to punch a guy. Hey, what are you doing here?"

"Like everyone else. Trying to get my money back from that bastard."

"I mean," Edward explained, "what are you doing here with your ankle like that?"

"I can't leave." Amy, feeling dizzy with the exertion of standing for hours asked, "Would you mind if I just...?" Amy threw an arm around Edward's neck and leaned on him heavily.

At first Edward looked pleased, then alarmed. "Someone get a doctor." He lowered her nearly unconscious body gently to the ground, put his jacket under her head, and felt her forehead. "She's burning up," he said with alarm.

Silent Film Actress Lillian Gish

Edward took the ice he was using on his eye and rubbed the inside of her forearm with it.

"Maybe she's got flu!" The matronly woman responded immediately and took a step back.

The nearby crowd responded in turn. "Flu? Someone has flu? Stand back! That lady has flu! Half my family died of the flu. Get away from her!" In panic, the crowd moved back clearing a circle around Amy and Edward.

"I've got to get her out of here," Edward told himself as he looked around trying to decide just how he would do that.

Meanwhile, inside Ponzi's office in the Hanover Bank, Cassullo sat across from him at the huge desk.

"Ya wanted to see me?" Cassullo began.

"What are you trying to do to me?" Ponzi asked. "I've got to put a stop to this." Ponzi put a large handful of certificates on the desktop.

"What are those?" Cassullo asked innocently.

"Don't pretend you don't know what they are. They're counterfeits, and not very good ones. You really should get a better printer if you're going to bother to cheat me. You signed them. You've been taking advantage of me you goddamn thief."

"That's a laugh. Isn't that like the pot calling the kettle black?" Cassullo flashed a victorious smile.

"What's your point?" asked Ponzi.

Cassullo shook his head and rolled his eyes, as if Ponzi were dense. "Isn't it about time for you to cut and run for it?"

"I'm not going anywhere. I told you from the very beginning, this is a legitimate business."

"Let me see if I got this right," Cassullo said. "You've got millions — in cash — and instead of bailing you plan to stick it out and give the money back to folks hand over fist?"

Ponzi sniffed. "All a criminal mind can think about is short-term profit."

"Better than a sharp stick in the eye."

"What you can't see is that if I wait this out, everyone will have confidence in me. It's an amazing business and I've only started making money."

"You're always full of big plans, but what about when they want to look at your books. What are you gonna do then Mr. Big Time Operator?"

"Something your petty little brain would never think of."

"I think you're bluffin'," Cassullo challenged. "I think you'll run for it."

"Think what you want. Just remember this; I own this bank. I don't have to steal anything from anybody. I've got a whole vault full of notes and securities people can look at. They're just sitting there waiting for me to show to anyone who wants to see. Including any auditors that might be interested."

"Well, that's way out of my league," Cassullo confessed. "Me, I'm blowin' town. Getting a bit too warm for me."

Ponzi picked up the counterfeit certificates and looked at the amounts of money involved in Cassullo's theft. "From the looks of it you've been dipping in pretty deep."

"Can't complain," Cassullo smiled.

"Get out of my sight," Ponzi ordered with disgust.

Chapter 32

The Fix

An indignant Ponzi strode into the office where Richard Grozier and the States Attorney Pelletier were smoking cigars.

"What the hell do you want?" was Ponzi's greeting.

"I don't believe you've been introduced," Richard said, rising from his seat. "Mr. Pelletier, this is Mr. Charles Ponzi. Mr. Ponzi, Mr. Pelletier, Attorney for the State of Massachusetts."

"Okay Pelletier, what do you want?" asked Ponzi.

"Personally, I'd love to shut you down," Pelletier confessed.

"You have no reason to do that. I've never dealt with a single customer with anything but the utmost honesty. No one has lost a nickel here. No one has any reason to complain."

"That would appear to be true. Nevertheless, I'm not here because of a complaint. I'm here to discover the answer to one simple question."

"Enlighten me," demanded Ponzi.

"Mr. Ponzi, are you solvent?"

"Of course I am," huffed Ponzi.

"Can you convince me?" asked Pelletier.

"Is there any doubt?" asked Ponzi.

"A great deal of doubt," asserted Pelletier.

"Some people are never satisfied. What does it take in your case?"

"There must be an audit of your books," suggested Pelletier.

"An audit? Look, I can show you assets in the multi-millions. Here are just a few of my accounts." Ponzi opened a drawer and pulled out a stack of bankbooks.

"I need more than that. I need a complete accounting of all your records, all the obligations to your investors as well as your assets. The options are to cooperate or I'll have to shut you down permanently."

"That's just not possible. How can there be an audit when there is so much going on? I'm taking in and paying out hundreds of thousands of dollars, if not millions, every day. And most of the transactions are small... twenty dollars, or fifty, maybe as much as a hundred," Ponzi protested.

"Mr. Ponzi, aren't you interested in knowing whether you are solvent or not?"

"You'll wreck me!" Ponzi yelled. "You simply cannot be allowed to ruin my reputation when you have no reason to suspect me. Are you prepared to compensate me for the damage to my business and my reputation?"

"Your reputation is not my problem," said Pelletier.

"What happens when you audit my books and find that I am solvent? Would you call off your dogs?" asked Ponzi.

"We'd have to," confessed Pelletier. "You'd be untouchable. We'd have no choice but to allow you to continue to operate."

"Just think of it," suggested Richard. "A clean bill of health from the States Attorney. That would be impressive. It would be like having their blessing. What a fantastic way to put all the ugly rumors to rest. New investors would flock to you in droves."

"Interesting," considered Ponzi who liked the possibilities that being legitimized in that way might offer him. "Tell me more."

"You'll have to close down for a few days and supply us with all your documents of course," explained Pelletier.

"That's not necessarily a bad thing," Richard reminded Ponzi. "After all, if the States Attorney closes you down for an audit, no one will be able to take money out, but they can hardly blame you."

"But....but...." said Ponzi, who prepared to launch a rebuttal.

"And refusing to take investor's money while you are being vindicated can only whet their appetite," continued Richard.

They all laughed.

"The blame will be entirely yours Mr. Pelletier," said Ponzi, serious again. "I'll let the world know I was against the plan but had no choice."

"Indeed," confirmed Pelletier. "You don't have a choice."

Richard smiled broadly. "It looks like a terrible miscarriage of justice to me. I must inform the press. The public will be very upset when they learn how you're being mistreated."

Ponzi smiled in return.

"We're ready to begin mistreating you immediately," said Pelletier.

Early the following morning the crowds showed up at the office of the Securities Exchange Company as usual. However now a sign on the door read: "Until further notice, the offices of the Securities Exchange Company are closed for audits."

Under the official sign, a handwritten sign reads, "Your money is safely earning interest. Mr. Charles Ponzi, President, Securities Exchange Company." Ponzi had signed with a flourish.

The throngs in the hallway read the sign with dismay, but word got out quickly that there was an audit going on, and their money was safe.

Inside the main office a team of eight auditors, dressed in black suits with visors sat at tables piled with certificates, receipts and comptroller's calculating machines.

Richard was sitting at the desk in the front office when Lucy entered.

"It's so quiet," said Lucy who'd grown accustomed to the bustle and near chaos she'd managed daily for weeks.

"Please have a seat," suggested Richard and Lucy sat in the chair across from him.

"I just feel so useless sitting around like this," Lucy complained.

"It must seem strange to you," said Richard as he considered her dilemma.

"I need something to keep my mind occupied," said Lucy.

"Yes! You need something to do, something dreadfully complex and very, very disorganized to put you right," suggested Richard.

"Yes, that's what I need," said Lucy sounding genuinely depressed.

"May I suggest?" asked Richard.

"Sure." Lucy looked a bit hopeful.

Richard, with a very serious tone began to outline the plan. "I think you should manage me. I'm a mess."

"You?" asked Lucy, confused.

Small Talk

"Oh yes. Isn't it obvious? I'm oozing with disorder and mayhem. I need someone who loves a challenge to take me on. For starters, I have never, not once in my life, balanced my checkbook."

"Really?" asked an incredulous Lucy. "That's easy. Anyone can balance a checkbook."

"I can't." said Richard proudly. "And I won't make it easy for you either! I'll thwart you in every way possible. I'll rant, I'll protest, I'll lose deposit slips. I'll leave my dirty laundry all over the bills and I'll never make a single payment on time without your capable supervision. You'll really have your hands full.

"Really? Lucy asked, standing, walking around Richard as if assessing him afresh.

"My own father will be happy to vouch for what an incompetent I am."

"Hmmm," thought Lucy. "You could have potential."

"A true fixer-upper," Richard stood up, arms open, and beamed a self-satisfied smile.

"But this is only a temporary lull while the audit is going on," Lucy pointed out.

"I'm not sure about that. Didn't you see the newspaper this morning?" asked Richard.

"Why? What's happened?" Lucy asked with alarm.

"Richard spread the Boston Post on the desk showing a blaring headline declaring: "Ponzi, Canadian Criminal Record." There is a sizeable mug shot showing young Ponzi and Edward Dunn's byline.

"Oh my god!" The devastation is painted on Lucy's shocked face.

"I'm sorry, Lucy. Truly sorry," Richard said and put his arms around poor Lucy who lost her battle with the tears.

Charles Ponzi's Canadian Mug Shot

Chapter 33

Breakdown

Amy Newly lay in bed, alone in a hospital room crying. Her leg with the twisted ankle was elevated on pillows. Diane and Eduardo entered the room unannounced and stood side-by-side next to her bed. Amy wiped her eyes and blew her nose. Diane handed her sister a small bouquet. Amy let the flowers drop on the bed.

"The nurse says your fever is down," said Diane. "Are you feeling any better?"

"A little. But then I saw this." Amy showed Diane the front-page newspaper story about Ponzi's criminal past. She cried again, speaking through her sobs. "The paper says he's a criminal. I've lost everything— everything — every bleeding dime."

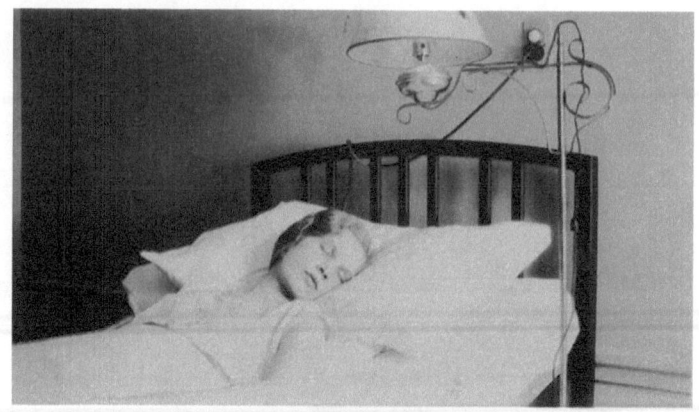

Woman in the Hospital

"Oh well," Diane said, straightening the covers a bit. "At least you didn't have that much to lose to begin with."

"That's not the point," Amy responded angrily. "It was everything I had. You, on the other hand, made money. It says here that the money the later investors, put in was used to pay the earlier investors, like you."

"I guess that means I was lucky," Diane said.

"I guess that means my money went to pay you," Amy said, glaring at her sister. "Is it really okay with you that you made lots of money at my expense and I lost everything?"

"You certainly can't hold me responsible for what happened," Diane replied defensively.

"Why not? Ponzi took my money and turned around and gave it to you. Besides, you were the one who told me to invest with him in the first place."

"Look Amy, I'm really sorry you lost your little nest egg, but that's not what we came here to talk about. We came to tell you that we're getting married and moving to Argentina."

"What do you mean?" Amy asked in alarm as the potential consequences dawned on her.

"We're leaving next week for Argentina."

"What about the dance studio?"

"We're closing it." Diane continued.

"What about me? What do you expect me to do?"

"It's not like you can dance anyway, not with your ankle like that. Besides we only gave you a job to try to help you in the first place," Diane confessed.

"So, what should I do now? How do I pay the hospital bill? Ask you for a loan? Did you think about that?" wondered Amy out loud.

"You have no idea how expensive it is to travel all the way to Argentina. Then we have all the wedding expenses to pay, not to mention our living expenses until Eduardo starts working."

"How can you do it? Just leave me like this?" The question just hung in the air.

Finally, Diane answered her sister. "Look Amy, you don't have to be so jealous just because I got lucky and you didn't."

Silent Film Actress Laura La Plante

"You think I envy you?" asked a now furious Amy as she sat up in bed. "You're not even close. I'm not jealous. It's worse than that: I'm horrified."

"Think about it," continued Amy. "If you leave and take everything with you, you'll never be able to face me again. You'll have to concoct some story about me — about how I deserve this because I'm foolish, or because I'm always the victim. You'll tell everyone that it was my own fault. Then you'll try to forget me."

"This is all Ponzi's fault, not mine," Diane objected.

"You're right. Ponzi is a bad man, a greedy man, and a terribly selfish human being. But now you're no different. Now you're just like he is. The bastard didn't just steal my money, he stole my sister."

Diane and Eduardo turned to leave and Amy threw the flowers at Diane. "Good-bye," she called out as they left. "Forever good-bye."

Alone again, Amy cried.

Chapter 34

Back Pedaling

Diane Newly was at home, filing her nails and speaking on the phone with her hairdresser.

"Yes I'm canceling my appointment. I'm canceling all my appointments. You sent me to that creep Ponzi. I never want to see you again. You'll be lucky if I don't sue you."

Diane's now former hairdresser was at the front desk of her salon. "Look, Miss Newly," she tried to explain. "I'm sorry but it ain't my fault the guy's a crook. I'm such a sap, I lost a hundred dollars myself."

The hairdresser slammed down the phone and returned to her workstation. The Bookie's girlfriend was in the chair sobbing.

"Bernie says he's gonna kill Ponzi if I don't get my money back. I gotta tell ya. I'm frightened for him."

"Who? You're frightened for Ponzi?" asked the hairdresser.

"No. For Bernie," the girlfriend replied.

Beauty Parlor

A few hours later, Bernie the Bookie and his girlfriend were in bed in a cheap hotel.

"I hate that little weasel," Bernie said angrily. "What a crook! Imagine him stealing from so many innocent people like that."

"But Bernie, you're a crook too!" said the girlfriend.

"Yeah, but not like that guy," Bernie explained.

The phone rang and Bernie answered it. "I hear you been lookin' for me," came the voice through the phone. "Yeah, can you believe it? Who woulda thought the guy was such a scum? ... Hey! Bernie! Relax! No, I like my face the way it is.... A whole grand? You want a take a grand outta my hide? Ouch! That's a tall order. Yeah, don't worry. I'll make it up to ya."

It's late afternoon, just the time when the commuters were heading to the train. The newspaper seller sees his regular, the pony player, heading his way and gets a copy of *The Boston Globe* folded and ready for him.

"Here's your paper Mac," smiles the news seller.

"Not interested," the pony player responded. "I gotta tip for *you* this time. You better cough up a grand by the end of the week or get outta town."

A few minutes later another regular shows up at the newsstand. The waitress from the lunch counter hands the seller a nickel.

"I'll take a Post," she says.

"We gotta talk," says the news seller. He grabs her wrist and maneuvers her to the side of the stand. "I need to borrow a grand. This is a life and death thing... all because of that bad tip you gave me about that Ponzi guy."

"You're kidding me!" the waitress told him. "I'm flat broke. I lost everything to Ponzi. I had to borrow a nickel for the goddamn paper. I lost my job because I was waiting in line to get my money back from that creep and I still lost everything. Now my landlord wants to evict me. I don't know what to do, but I can't take anymore."

The waitress is waiting on the sidewalk outside the Woolworths where she used to work at the lunch counter. It's raining and she's holding the newspaper over her head to fend off the raindrops. Finally, her old regular, the man she was waiting for, came out the door and she approached him. "Hey mister. You remember me?" she asked him.

The man stopped walking. "Yeah. You used to work here," he said plainly.

"Listen. You remember the tip you gave me? Invest with Ponzi you said."

"What's your point?" he asked suspiciously.

"It's all gone. Everything I had," she told him with a quiver in her voice full of pathos. "Please help me," she clutched his sleeve and begged.

"That's not my fault. Get away from me," he said, and shaking her hand from his sleeve, he turned and walked away.

The waitress pulled a knife from her purse and ran after him, violently stabbing him in the back. He stumbled, his face full of shock as he dropped to his knees on the wet pavement in front of the shoeshine stand, blood gushing onto the pavement from his wound.

Manzoni was sitting reading a newspaper and waiting for his turn for a shoeshine when a pedestrian in front of him, a familiar looking man, grabbed his paper and stared him in the face as he stumbled and fell bleeding to the ground.

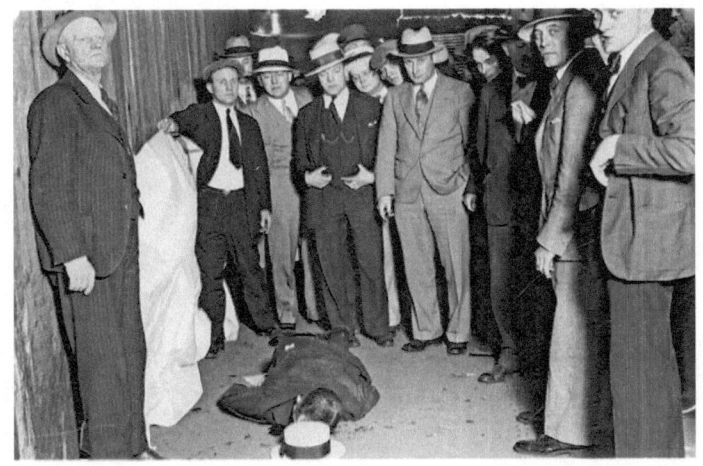

Street Crime Scene

The shoeshine boy ran to the fallen man, crouched at his side. "He's been stabbed," he yelled.

Manzoni was frantic. "We've gotta get help! I'll call the cops."

Manzoni ran down the street to the Gnecco's fruit market where Papa Gnecco was stacking apples. "Mr. Gnecco, you've gotta help! A man's been stabbed! He needs an ambulance! I need to use your phone to call the police!"

They both raced inside the tiny store and Papa handed Manzoni the phone. Manzoni dropped his newspaper on the top of the counter while he summoned the police. Papa Gnecco saw, for the first time, the front-page story with the mug shot of Ponzi and the headlined that blared about his criminal past.

"My poor Rose. My poor little girl," her father lamented. "Does she know?" he wondered.

Chapter 35

Poor Rose

The veranda in front of Ponzi's house in Lexington was filled with reporters and photographers yelling and banging on the door. After a few minutes, Imelda Ponzi opened the door a crack and looked out. The reporters yelled for Ponzi.

Imelda shook her head and motioned for them to leave.

"We need to talk to someone," said the nearest reporter. "Let us talk to Rose."

Imelda smiled when she recognized the name and closed the door. A silence fell over the occupants of the porch as they waited.

Slowly the door opened and the lovely, innocent Rose stepped outside nervously, clutching her shoulders and smiling shyly.

Reporters with Cameras

A reporter fired a question. "Mrs. Ponzi, were you aware of your husband's criminal background?"

Rose looked confused. Another reporter shoved a newspaper into her hands. "Did you know your husband was a crook in Canada?" came his question followed by a volley of questions from the other reporters.

Rose looked stricken. She gasped, dropped the newspaper and dropped to her knees, then to the floor in a dead faint. There was a flash from a camera. Then another. And another.

It was hours later, long after sundown, when Ponzi finally returned home to find his poor wife ill and in bed. He knelt beside her, explaining the part of his past that the newspaper had revealed.

"It was nothing Rose — just a youthful indiscretion. I'm not a criminal Rose. It could have happened to anyone."

"You were in jail," Rose whispered.

"It was a travesty of justice my dear, dear Rose. I was alone in a foreign land."

"You should have told me. I could have forgiven you."

"Don't worry Rose," he assured her. "It's okay. Everything will be okay."

Car horns were heard outside and the doorbell rang and rang as they spoke.

Cars were parked on the lawn with bright headlights pointed at the house. Reporters and photographers milled around on the porch. Ponzi finally stepped outside and was blinded by the glare. Microphones were thrust into his face. The game face reappeared.

"Gentlemen," Ponzi began, "I do hope you'll understand. My lovely wife needs her sleep so I want to keep this brief. In typical fashion, The Boston Post has printed a misleading story about me. I want to assure my investors that I am not a crook. Yes, I served a brief period of incarceration over a decade ago due to mistakes I made in my youth. I served my time and like everyone else, I deserve a second chance. I want my investors to know they can trust me. I assure you that every nickel invested with me is safe. After all, if I really were a criminal I would have left the country with my millions long ago. All I want now is to put this upsetting episode behind me and get back to business. Good night and God bless America."

Ponzi's face was lit a blazing white by the flashes from the cameras.

Chapter 36

Just Borrowing

Ponzi paced behind his desk at the Hanover Bank. Chmielinski stood awaiting orders.

"I remind you. I have an important meeting at one," Ponzi told his employee.

"Are the auditors giving their report?" asked Chmielinski nervously.

"It hardly matters," Ponzi said. "Nevertheless, I want you to make sure the vault is open and I want you to wait there for me."

"What do you need?" Chmielinski asked. "Perhaps I can have it ready for you."

"Just have the vault open and be there." Ponzi glared.

At precisely one, the auditors took their seats at the long table in the Hanover boardroom. Seconds later, Ponzi entered the room and marched to his seat at the head of the table.

"Gentlemen," Ponzi began. "I trust you've seen everything you need to see."

"I'm satisfied," said States Attorney Pelletier, who would act as the spokesperson for the auditors.

"Good. I'll reopen the business immediately," Ponzi announced.

"Mr. Ponzi. Aren't you interested in knowing what we discovered during our audit of your business?" asked Pelletier.

"Not really." Ponzi stated matter-of-factly. "I just want you to clear my name. I've got a business to run."

Ponzi leaned back in his chair, like a ruling potentate, and lit a cigar.

"As a matter or fact, I'm putting together a group of investors to purchase ten thousand surplus warships," he continued, taking a puff on the cigar. "We're going to refit them as showrooms to exhibit American-made goods and send them all over the world."

Ponzi smiled for the auditors. "This is going to be big!" he claimed. "When customers want our merchandise, we'll just pull the stock right out of the holds of the ships! No further shipping charges!"

The auditors were stone faced.

"Then," Ponzi continued, "we'll have buyers aboard every ship looking to buy the best foreign-made goods. We'll refill the ships with merchandise to bring back to the American market to sell."

Again, there was no reaction from his audience.

"And best of all, this business is so profitable even you boys will want a piece of it."

"I'm afraid not," said Pelletier.

"Suit yourself. I don't need you."

"You misunderstand," said Pelletier. "We can't let you reopen the Securities Exchange Company. You're overdrawn to the tune of forty thousand dollars."

"Are you sure?" asked Ponzi.

"You're bankrupt Mr. Ponzi."

"I am?" smiled a relaxed Mr. Ponzi, blowing a cloud of smoke in Pelletier's direction.

"We're going to have to close you down."

"I very much doubt that I'm bankrupt. You've obviously made a mistake. I don't think you've considered all of my assets."

"Here is a list of all of the assets we've included in our audit, said Pelletier, offering Ponzi a copy. "If there are any assets missing, we'd be happy to know about them."

"Let me see." Ponzi reviewed the list briefly and then looked up.

"Gentlemen, I'm sure I'll be able to clear up this matter very easily. I hope you'll excuse me for a minute while I collect a few papers. Meanwhile, I've taken the liberty of ordering a bit of a luncheon for you to enjoy."

Serving Luncheon

Ponzi opened the doors to the boardroom and two waiters entered pushing carts of steaming food and immediately began serving the auditors.

"The brandy and cigars are on the sideboard," Ponzi said as he quietly slipped away.

Ponzi found Chmielinski pacing in front of the vault, its door ajar.

"Come here," he ordered Chmielinski. "Help me get my hands on some good securities."

Bank Vault

Ponzi rifled through files in a sturdy metal cabinet inside the vault, grabbing documents and scrutinizing them quickly.

"Are you sure those are what you want?" asked Chmielinski. "Those certificates belong to bank customers. We're just holding them as security on loans and such."

"I'm not going to steal them. I just need to borrow them for a few minutes," Ponzi explained. "I want to show them to the idiot auditors and then put them back."

"That doesn't sound like such a good idea," said Chmielinski.

"Of course it's a good idea. Don't worry. I'll bring them back when I'm done with them."

Richard Grozier and Edward Dunn suddenly appeared from behind the cabinet.

"It really is a good idea, isn't it Edward?" asked Richard.

"A very good idea," Edward agreed. "Entirely sneaky, underhanded and illegal, but very clever."

"You aren't authorized to be here," Ponzi threatened. "This is none of your affair. Call security Chmielinski!"

"No, but it is my affair," came a voice and suddenly Pelletier appeared at the entrance of the vault. "Not only are you bankrupt, it appears you are trying to commit a fraud."

"I've done nothing," claimed Ponzi as he dropped the securities he was holding.

"Caught red handed I'd say. Take him away," Pelletier ordered and two police officers appeared to do just that.

Ponzi walked out of the bank vault between two police officers.

As the policemen escorted the still smiling Ponzi to a nearby paddy wagon, a woman approached him and yelled. "I hate you. I spit on you. I curse you, you thief. You stole everything I had."

Charles Ponzi with the Auditors

Ponzi did not respond and continued to smile.

A throng of young men was waiting at the curb in front of the Hanover Bank and cheered when they saw him. Ponzi lifted his hat and waved to them.

One of the admirers cupped his hands and yelled, "Don't let them stop you Mr. Ponzi. The little guys of this world need a man like you to look up to."

Another of his buddies agreed. "We support you Mr. Ponzi! Don't stop fighting!"

"I have no intention of stopping my fight against this injustice," Ponzi told the policemen who didn't care either way.

"I have my rights!" said Ponzi. "This is America."

Chapter 37

Special Edition

The street was covered with snow. A taxi pulled to the curb and Richard Grozier stepped out, tuxedo in disarray, vest unbuttoned, bowtie untied. He attempted to pull himself together as he ran up the steps and rushed through the door.

Lucy was waiting for Richard inside the lobby. She was elegantly dressed in an evening gown.

"Hurry. You're late," Lucy urged.

"How would you know it was me if I wasn't late?" smiled Richard.

"You're a bad boy Richard Grozier," Lucy said as she tied his tie and straightened his jacket. "Let's go!"

Richard and Lucy were the last arrivals in a grand auditorium filled with people in formal dress. They took their seats next to Amy Newly and Edward Dunn. Edward's arm was around Amy's shoulders. Edward shook Richard's hand.

The four watched the stage where, from a podium, a presenter spoke. "This year's Pulitzer Prize for Public Service is awarded to Mr. Richard Grozier and Mr. Edward Dunn of The Boston Post for exposing the operations of Charles Ponzi in a series of investigative reports that led to his arrest."

The crowd applauded enthusiastically. Richard and Edward shook hands and embraced the women. As the applause increased, the pair of men stood and bowed to the crowd, then each other.

After the award presentation, the foursome stepped outside where the snow was still lightly falling and a newsboy was selling *The Boston Post*.

"Post Heah! Special edition. Big prizewinners. Read all about it."

"Give me a couple of those," Richard told the newsboy. He paid for the papers and handed them to the young women.

"Wow, a Special Edition? At ten o'clock at night? They even have a story about the two of you on the front page — with photos," said Amy.

"How'd they do that so fast?" asked Lucy.

"I am the publisher after all," bragged Richard.

"We're very fast. We're so fast we can report the news before it happens," claimed Edward.

"That's not possible," said Amy.

"Oh yes it is. Isn't that right Richard?"

"Of course," Richard agreed. "For example, I believe the story on page sixteen, right-hand column, above the fold is breaking as we speak."

The women opened their papers to page sixteen. The men looked over their shoulders.

"See. There it is," Edward pointed out. "Post reporter Edward Dunn announces engagement to Miss Amy Newly."

"Oh my God!" yelled Amy!

Surprised Couple

"Amy, I've been in love with you from the moment I first held your-ankle. Would you please, please do me the great honor of marrying me?" asked Edward.

Amy and Lucy screamed with delight. Amy tried to recover her dignity.

"According to the Special Edition, I accepted, and I do accept, I do. I will marry you!" she laughed as she threw her arms around Edward.

Lucy and Richard cheered as the couple kissed.

"But is that all the article had to say?" asked Richard.

"Let me see," said Lucy. She opened the paper again and read. "Continued on page seventeen, it says."

Lucy turned the page and read. "Furthermore, his friend and colleague, the Post's Publisher, Richard Grozier will be joining Dunn at the altar with his own bride, Miss Lucy Melli."

"Is this true Richard?" asked Lucy, eyes opened wide.

"Yes, of course. You have Boston's most reputable newspaper's word on it. Just watch." Richard took Lucy's hand and placed it on his heart. "My lovely Lucy, you really are the love of my life. I desperately need your vast capabilities. Will you please, please manage me the rest of our lives?"

"You're serious?" she asked.

"I am."

"But this is such a big decision— a really important decision, and I'm such a bad judge of character. I didn't do well with Mr. Ponzi did I? I was such an idiot." Tears began to flow. Richard put his arm around her and she leaned her head onto his shoulder.

"You can't blame yourself. He fooled me too," assured Amy.

"Hell, he fooled nearly everyone in Boston," said Edward.

"I love you Richard, and I really want to marry you, but I need to be sure. So, give me ninety days…"

"And I can collect with interest?" asked Richard, beaming.

"Deal," said Lucy.

Richard and Lucy shook hands then joined the other couple in an embrace.

The End

Bride & Groom

PostScript

After the arrest of Charles Ponzi and a long trial, he served over ten years in prison during which his mother died and Rose waited. But his life as a swindler didn't end in Boston. His further misadventures included selling swampland in Florida and deportation to Italy where he worked for the brutal dictator, Mussolini. Rose followed him for many years, although even she left him in the end. He died alone as a pauper in a hospital in Brazil, leaving only the seventy-five dollars used to bury him.

About the Author

M.R. Paxson (Monica Rix) began her professional life in publishing as a book designer. She learned how to write by entering the corrections editors made on the manuscripts of the books she was producing. Her first book, *The Fabulous Money-Making Garage Sale Kit*, co-authored with her sister Diana, was a media hit and was featured on Good Morning America, CBS This Morning and on hundreds of radio programs. Her second, a serious science book, *Dead Mars, Dying Earth*, was co-authored with Dr. John Brandenburg. It was first published in the U.K and was featured on the BBC. It tackled the issue of global warming from a planetary science perspective and was the winner of a Benjamin Franklin Award and achieved best-seller status on Amazon. Her well-reviewed memoir, *Talking2Trees & Other True Transdimensional Tales* tells stories about synchronicities and other unlikely events. *Ponzi: The Prince of Pi Alley* was originally written as a screenplay that was optioned in 2009, perhaps the worst year in Hollywood history. A U.S. citizen, M.R. lives and works in Cuernavaca, Mexico.

About Relentlessly Creative Books

Relentlessly Creative Books™ offers an exciting new publishing option for authors. Our "middle path publishing" approach includes many of the advantages of both traditional publishing and self-publishing without the drawbacks. For more information and a complete online catalog of our books, please visit us online.

For readers, join our Readers Group. Register online and enjoy free eBooks, sneak previews on new releases, book sales, author interviews, book reviews, reader surveys and online events with Authors.

RelentlesslyCreativeBooks.com
books@relentlesslycreative.com.